"HOW COME YOU'RE HERE NOW?"

Knossos' eyes were rock-steady on mine as he answered. "We are here because we lost the war, and we must now do the best we can. Like you, little Shade."

The lion man and the wolf man stopped eating, and for a moment the table was very quiet. Too quiet. The only sound was my heart beating. Knossos was seated across from me, but he also seemed to be farther away; and instead of rags I saw metal and leather on his huge body. The wolf man and lion man wore space armor. They were younger, strong; and Knossos, standing at their center, leading them into battle, was their king. Behind them through the mist was a wonderful city—

Knossos touched my shoulder. "Shade." His voice thrummed in my ears like a war drum. "Are you all right?"

SENSATIONAL SCIENCE FICTION

SHADE

Emily Devenport

A ROC BOOK

ROC
Published by the Penguin Group
Penguin Books USA Inc., 375 Hudson Street,
New York, New York 10014, U.S.A.
Penguin Books Ltd, 27 Wrights Lane,
London W8 5TZ, England
Penguin Books Australia Ltd, Ringwood,
Victoria, Australia
Penguin Books Canada Ltd, 10 Alcorn Avenue,
Toronto, Ontario, Canada M4V 3B2
Penguin Books (N.Z.) Ltd, 182–190 Wairau Road,
Auckland 10, New Zealand

Penguin Books Ltd, Registered Offices:
Harmondsworth, Middlesex, England

First published by Roc, an imprint of New American Library,
a division of Penguin Books USA Inc.

First Printing, December, 1991
10 9 8 7 6 5 4 3 2 1

Roc is a trademark of New American Library,
a division of Penguin Books USA Inc.

PRINTED IN THE UNITED STATES OF AMERICA

For Charlie Ryan, who let me get my foot in the door, and Margaret Devenport, who paid the light bill.

Knossos told me I should keep a journal. I asked him where he thought I was going to get pen and paper. "Probably the same place you get food and loki," he said. Like it's supposed to be easy or something. So here I sit going scribble scribble while he's off doing God Knows What.

One thing I'd rather be doing. I'd rather be at the pits. But Knossos borrowed all the money we won together that last time. Don't get the wrong idea. He didn't tinker me over. You wouldn't think that if you knew the elephant man. Besides, I can spare the cash, and I sure know how to live without it. I just had a good meal, got two sticks of loki in my pocket, and from where I'm sitting now I can hear the hot music pouring out of Club Draggit. I feel as good as you would if you were sitting in an overstuffed chair in your living room. Maybe better, because I'm young and skinny and have the hottest haircut in town.

I went through a lot for this haircut. Yesterday I was sitting in the barber's chair, and his hand kept darting toward my breasts, like it was some animal with a mind of its own. He's grinning and cutting and darting. "You live near here?" he asks me. What a tinker-brain.

"No," I say, "I've got an apartment in the Spacer Sector." I wish.

"Maybe I could stop in and see you sometime," he says, proving that he's not listening.

"You already got paid," I said. "I scoped your partner for you, and now you know he's cheating you blind. You think he might want to know some stuff about you?"

He didn't answer, and for several minutes his hand stayed away from my tits. But eventually it came back again, twice as curious. This nonsense made the haircut last much longer than it had to; and let me tell you, I didn't enjoy sitting in that chair with his sweat dripping on me, because it was eighty percent humidity in there when it was only seventy percent outside, and he had more flying bugs than I've ever seen collected in one place before—all of whom were at least as interested in my nose as he was in my tits.

I waited for the last snip and got up. I whipped off the bib and gave him a look at my Deadtown rag-wraps to remind him what I am. But he just didn't get it. He tried to block my way. I gave his foot a nice dent with my boot heel.

"No tip for you," I said on my way out. Guess I'll have to get a new barber.

But he cut my hair just the way I like it, shaved on the sides like the pit fighters. Most Deadtowners just hack their hair off with their knives, but I'm vain.

Once out on the sidewalk I took the time to brush the freshly snipped hair off my neck. Had to bend over to do that, and my shades fell off. I picked them up, straightened, and looked right into the eyes of a Lyrri-dog who was standing

across the street. He got a good look at me before
I got the shades back in place.

I moved off casually. There are plenty of ways
to lose a dog in Midtown, what with all the
demolition and construction that's going on, so I
wasn't panicked yet. The Lyrri-dog had this little smile on his pretty face; the kind of smile
even the most chance-loving gambler on planet
Z'taruh would recognize as a bad proposition.
Lyrri love torture more than they do roulette—
and they love that a lot.

I didn't glance over my shoulder as I walked
along, though I sure felt like it. I turned a corner
and wove my way through the ruins of an old
pre-fab until I thought I was behind him, and
then I looked. He was just walking down the
street, stretching those long, graceful legs of his,
but I scoped him anyway—though not too deep. I
didn't want to fall over or anything if his mind
was too creepy. I just fluttered over him like a
moth.

And he was something. He was the Big Decep-
tion, just like all Lyrri, so gentle looking. Mr.
Gracious. He smiled at the people who passed
him, and those that didn't know any better smiled
back. Then he would touch them, all casual and
friendly, like a brother or something, and continue on as if he were just out for a stroll. I bet
later they find bruises where those long fingers
found sensitive spots they didn't even know they
had.

He crossed the street and walked into Mer-
chant's Square, one of those new shopping plazas
that try so pathetically to make Midtown seem
more like the Spacer Sector. I was shaking by the
time he had put more space between us, because

I could feel him searching through my fluttery link. I went a little deeper, and the Lyrri's form blurred, became something more feral.

He could have killed anyone on that street without sweating—any of the other dogs, human or even the Q'rin with their rock-hard bodies, even if they had their force-guns drawn. And he wasn't even armed. And I thought to myself that this is why Runaways, Babies, and Skids don't last more than a few years on this planet. Because there are predators hunting here.

I pulled away from the touch and my eyes went back to normal. There he was again, just walking and smiling, looking lean and sharp. Silver threads caught the sunlight from the depths of the black cloth that hugged his body so tight it looked painted on. A lot of humans wish they looked like the Lyrri look. Me, I think their skin is too white. Lots of people like that, though. Stupid people. Like the people who didn't have the sense to stay more than an arm's length away from the Lyrri-dog as he strolled into the crowd of shoppers and disappeared.

Maybe he was just trying to make the same kind of deal with me the barber had, but I don't want anything to do with him. I was glad when he was gone.

And I put him out of my mind in favor of more important things. Like lunch, which I was already late for. I headed straight for the fast-food stalls, which nest right at the juncture of Midtown, Deadtown, and the Spacer Sector. Meat and grease smells wafted over to me, temporarily chasing away the Z'taruhn smells of smoke, garbage, sewage, and mildew. My nose was in Nirvana.

Deadtowners stalked in and out of the crowd like multicolored mummies, rag-wrapped like me, to show their separateness and independence. I joined the hunt, slipping in among the mass of tinkers who like to stuff themselves there. I got some ugly looks from the old tinkers, who just hate the idea of hungry Deadtowners parting them with their money before they can spend it on casinos/booze/hookers/Babies and/or their own pathetic little families.

I wormed here and there, back and forth, looking for unguarded food and pockets. Since the renovation project started in Midtown, there's been an influx of tinkers from off-planet—nice new unsuspecting meat. I wallowed in among them. I picked up on some gossip, too.

"Mecham's hiring for that job in the Northern Sector," said one old fat character. He was working his way through *two* meatball subs, but he only had his hands on one of them.

"Shit, you mean Outskirts," said his skinnier friend, who had the Avocado Special clutched firmly in his paws. "They're always threatening to clean that up. Never happen."

"They're doin' it." Fatso took another bite of luscious, yummy meatball.

"Never."

"Uh huh. They already rented supplies and equipment from Atlas. My cousin Doug saw the invoices. And he's already drawn two weeks pay. And you know what?"

What? I wondered as I moved behind and to the left of him.

"Mecham is only taxing forty percent out of Doug's check."

"No way."

"Yes, sir. And he's gettin' good solid work—forty to sixty hours a week, union pay. No shit."

Skinny chewed his sandwich for a minute and thought about that. Meanwhile, Fatso was about halfway through his first sub. I would have to move soon. I was so intent on those meatballs, somebody groped my butt and I didn't even care.

"Wait a minute," Skinny says. "Northern Sector. That's Q'rin territory. No fuckin' way, man."

"Why not?"

"Because they're takin' over the city, that's why not. If they get much farther, they're gonna be callin' *all* the shots. They already control all the banks anyway, you know."

Fatso just grunted, and that's how I knew he was on to me. No tinker would pass up the chance to complain about the Z'taruhn banks, not with the inflation rate around here. Especially an old-timer like this guy, who knows he's stuck on this planet for good.

"Fuckin' 'towner get the hell away from my butt before I shove my fist down your goddam throat!" Fatso bellowed in my general direction, but I was already moving before the first syllable. I didn't take it personally. It's just business.

Besides, it isn't my fault the tinkers get sucked dry by the banks and then lose what's left to the casinos. Lots of people are stuck here, and not all of us because we owe money. You can't owe what you don't have. So when I saw some greenhorn walk to a table with the biggest sandwich ever conceived, and then *leave* it there so he could get more mustard, I didn't hesitate. I took a big bite out of it as I walked away with it, so everyone would know it was mine.

But I wasn't the only one who had spotted that

sandwich. Some skinny kid shadowed me out of the stalls.

"Hand it over, bitch," he snarled.

I took another big bite.

"I bet you sell your cunt when no one's looking," he said. "Bet you sucked that tinker's cock to get that sub."

I laughed in his face, then slipped out my knife and gave him The Look. The Look says, "Are you willing to die for this (fill in the blank)? I am." I took a third bite of the sandwich until he backed away. He had that thin, crazed look of a Deadtowner who isn't going to make it. He'd either start selling his ass on a street corner, or he'd starve. I wondered if I shouldn't give him part of the sandwich after all ...

Who the hell am I kidding? I didn't think about that at all while I was eating the sandwich. I just thought of it now. I was trying to picture him while I wrote this, remembering all the things I had scoped out of him. Makes my stomach cramp up all over again with all that hunger and anger, and I almost feel sorry for him. But at the time, it just made me want to hold on to the sandwich tighter.

That's why it's not a good idea to scope people too deep—the physical effect, I mean. Too disturbing. Usually when I scope I just take everything I know about people and calculate the odds on what they're going to do next. I calculated that the kid would probably die. I didn't have any more time to waste on him. I only care about me and Knossos.

I must be getting tired, because three more songs have come crashing and banging out of Draggit's since I wrote that last part. I've been trying to decide where to sleep tonight. Salvation Army always has a cot to spare. Or I could check out the Baby School. But I don't want to hassle with the Babysitters. They don't like it when freeloaders take advantage of their accommodations. And the Q'rin-dogs are always coming down on that place, like they believe they really are the police instead of just armed thugs. So I think I'll sleep in the hidey-hole tonight.

I'll be sleeping safe and sound, and no one will bother me. No pimps or tinkers or dogs. Or other Deadtowners. Not even that Lyrri-dog.

I hope he's not after me.

Woke up with dawn leaking through the cracks in the shutters. Dreamed all night about my mother and sister, so of course they were the only things I could think of when I was trying to get back to sleep. Feel like I've been worked over with a big stick.

I don't know why I waste my time chewing over old stuff. I used to blame my mom for screwing up, but in the last couple of years I've seen how complicated life can be. Now I don't have anyone to blame, and it really pisses me off.

Besides, she really tried. "We are upper-middle class people," she used to tell me, especially after Dad left, like she was trying to convince herself as well as me. "We have things in our home from all over the world. We have an appreciation for art and music, *and we are educated.*" Unfortunately, we weren't financially upper class, though Mom tried to make it look that way.

Mom's a concert pianist, one of the best on Earth. Katie and I sometimes fought when she was trying to practice. Once, when Mom was in the living room plowing through Rachmoninov's "Third Piano Concerto" for an upcoming concert, Katie and I had a blow-up about who was going to get the last Chocolate Doodle Snack Cake. "You're too fat anyway," Katie said, as she pulled the cake out of its wrapper and put her fingerprints all over it.

But it wasn't the remark that got to me. It was when I tried to get the snack cake away from her and she squished it. Cake and cream filling squirting from between her fingers like popped zit. I punched her in the face.

She responded by throwing the fish bowl at me. I guess adrenalin gave her the extra strength. It broke as I deflected it with my arm, and rained glass and water on a painting a friend of my mom's did for her in college. My arm was cut open, but I was horrified about the painting.

"Look what you did to Mom!" I shrieked, and the fight escalated to global thermonuclear warfare.

By the time we were finished, the contents of the refrigerator were all over the walls and us, Katie and I were covered with blood and bruises, and Mom was locked in her bedroom, crying.

Katie retreated to her own bathroom to lick her wounds, throwing me a "now look what you've done" look before she slammed the door shut. But I was four years older, and I had a better understanding of semantics.

I started to clean the place up, keeping my ear out for Mom. She sobbed in her room for hours. Finally, I heard the door click, and she came out. I tried to talk to her, but a feeble, "Sorry, Mom," was all I could come up with. Her eyes didn't even focus on me, and that was when I learned the great cosmic Sometimes Sorry Doesn't Fix It law

Mom headed straight for the hall closet and got out her suitcases. Then she went back to her room. It took my dazed brain a moment to figure out what that meant, and I ran for the door just as she was about to close it. We had a struggle as she tried to force the door closed and I blocked it with my body. Finally Mom started to cry again, and gave up trying to keep me out of the room. She laid her suitcases on the bed, then went to her closet and started to pack.

As she packed her bags, I unpacked them. It was almost funny, the two of us going back and forth. While we worked, I begged her not to go. "Please, Mom. Give me another chance. I'll clean up the mess. Please, Mom." Over and over.

How strange it all would have looked to Knossos, that unhappy mess. That fear of abandonment, the pulling and tugging and straining and pleading. Aesopian elephant men always leave home at an early age, in search of their own destinies. The only hint I've ever had of familial sentiments on his part was when he and I got drunk together once, and I let it slip that my parents had left me when I was a kid. He put his massive arm around my shoulder and patted me gently. "They shouldn't have done that, Shade," he said. "You are a good daughter."

Eventually, Mom gave up trying to pack her bags. She was all cried out. She still wouldn't look at me. She lay down on her bed and went to sleep.

I took her bags and hid them in the attic. Then I spent the rest of the night and most of the next day cleaning up the mess Katie and I had made.

We never wrecked the house like that again, but the packing and unpacking continued. I got to be very good at sensing when Mom was about to leave. I always tried to head her off, but eventually I realised it was inevitable.

Maybe I wouldn't be as good at scoping if it weren't for Mom.

Everything comes back to that. The thing that kept me alive for so long is getting me into trouble now. Or maybe I just shouldn't have scoped the elephant man. He showed me ways to use my talent I never dreamed of.

If I could find Knossos, maybe we could win enough money to get off Z'taruh. At the pits. It's the only game I know I can win for sure—except maybe poker, where I can scope people while they read their cards. I tried to tell Knossos how good we could be together, but I never knew if he believed me. That elephant face was always the hardest to read.

Now I would be happy if I could just catch a glimpse of it.

I fell asleep again after all. I guess I bored myself to death. Loki always gives me a serious case of blabber-brain.

When I finally got started, I felt like the day had left me behind. I missed the only cool period Z'taruh has: the early morning, when the temperature gets down to a nice seventy-five degrees, though the humidity stays the same.

I cruised the fast-food stalls with pathetic results. When noon limped past and things didn't get any better, I wandered over to the Salvation Army to see what was cooking there.

I could have gone for pancakes and ham. What I got was hot gruel. But they had some nice biscuits to go with it. I had hoped Knossos might be there. But not today. So I sat with Mira and Snag and listened to Snag complain. He poked me when he noticed I had tuned him out.

"You still looking for Knossos?" he said. "You need to mind your own business."

"I do mind my own business," I said, pointedly. But it went right past him.

"Why you always chasing after him? He's important person. He's not got time for you."

"Just forget it," I said. I didn't want Knossos to hear I wanted to find him because, perversely, I was afraid that would just keep him away.

"You losing your touch, Shade," said Snag. "Lean, young Deadtowner like you hanging out with old Skids and begging food." He clicked his forked tongue against his fangs. "Too bad. Thought you the toughest kid around."

He was just running his mouth as usual, but it got under my skin. I choked down the rest of the gruel and walked out of there before I could scream at him. I just hated the fact that some green thing that likes to sleep on river bottoms was telling me this shit.

But it's true. I am losing it. I never had to beg food before, at least not after I learned the ropes here. What if word got out? You get your butt fucked at the first sign of weakness.

So I decided to head over to the Baby School, to prove to them and myself that I'm still Shade. They can damn well share their food with me. Loki too, if they have any. I've decided to spend the night there, too. Don't need a hidey-hole.

I guess it's a good thing I went to the Baby School when I did. Otherwise I wouldn't know what finks Lilo and Stone are. Guess that's what you should expect from a couple of Scarbabies. I saw them talking to that Lyrri-dog outside the front door. I hid in the doorway of the building two lots down and watched them, silently thanking the Midtown Construction Project for providing me with so much Shade-sized cover. The Lyrri paid them, but I don't think he was buying their bodies. Lyrri don't like their victims to be too willing.

They talked some more, and then he headed up the street in my direction. I pressed myself flat until he had passed me and didn't breathe until he turned the corner. Then I had a talk with myself.

I needed to find out what they had told him, but I was scared. Hate to admit it. Maybe I shouldn't fight it—the fear, I mean. Keeps you on your toes.

Anyway, I made myself go in. I entered through one of the bolt holes; made it a point to find out where every one of those things were long ago. Sauntered in past a couple of lookouts who were getting into each other. Or maybe they were just practicing for customers. That's why they call it the Baby School.

Don't qualify as a Baby myself anymore, now that my breasts (such as they are) finally grew. But I used to hang out there when I was new. Most Deadtowners think Babies are garbage because they sell their asses to get by instead of just stealing. Personally, I think we all start out the same way on this planet, as Runaways. So when I came into the dorm, everyone knew me and some were even glad to see me.

Of course, I could smell the place before I even entered. It has the most powerful urine smell you could ever imagine—the odor of unhappy children. It's one of the main reasons I don't like to sleep there any more than I have to—that and the Q'rin raids. Those fuckers actually go in there and kill children, as if they were cleaning out rats or something. Hence the bolt-holes. I only had to be there for one surprise raid to get the message.

"Shade!" My friend Ramona spotted me. "Get your ass over here!" She patted the dirty mattress she was sitting on.

It still sound funny to me to hear a nine-year-old talk that way, but I went over anyway.

"How about some of that loki you never seem to run out of?" I said. (It usually kills the pee smell.)

Ramona grinned and pulled out a stick. Insisted on lighting it for me and sliding it between my lips. I pulled on it and passed it back, keeping my eye on the door.

"The Q'rin came in here last night," Ramona said.

"Really?"

"Yeah. Tammy came running in here screaming 'Run! Run!' And we did, and Larry tripped when he was trying to get out the bolt-hole, and it was funny!"

I snorted. "That's a surprise." Ol' fat Larry is supposed to be looking after things and keeping this dump clean, but he spends most of his time helping himself to free Baby ass and trying to eat and drink himself to death. He's pretty typical of a Babysitter.

"Ernie and I were hiding in the boiler," Ramona said, "and we heard their big boots outside going CLOMP CLOMP CLOMP, BOOM BOOM BOOM, and we were *scaaaaarred*."

"I'll bet," I said. "They shoot anyone?"

"No. They haven't shot anyone in a couple of months, and ol' Larry says he thinks they're just trying to scare us. But he always runs the fastest!" She laughed, but I had a hard time laughing with her. Larry wasn't even around half the time anymore. The least the owners could do is to hire a couple of human-dogs to guard the place. Lord knows they buy enough Baby ass themselves.

After a while, Lilo and Stone came in. Immediately, the sex-babies began to fuss over them (except for Ramona, who had become involved in her coloring book). It was like watching Drones with Queen bees, stroking and patting and pushing sweets in their mouths.

Stone saw me first thing when he came in, and as usual his face didn't reveal anything. Or rather, his expression didn't. The scars and burns on his face say an awful lot. He never cries out. That's his speciality. So a look from me did nothing for him. He just let all those sex-babies, who only had to sell their asses because he was around to take the heavier trade, show him how grateful they were.

Lilo went all wiggly when he came into the room, pulled this way and that by the whims of everyone around him. He wasn't even aware I was there for the first fifteen minutes or so. When he finally saw me he got all breathless and made noises like, "Ummmmm, ohhhhh! Shade! Shadeshadeshade, Shaaaa—"

Little guy gives me the creeps.

Ramona giggled and passed me another loki stick. I sucked on it eagerly. I needed the drug to put a damper between me and Lilo. It does that for me, when I smoke enough of it. Maybe Lilo is a better scoper than I am, because as I was wondering for the millionth time if he was a boy or a girl, he immediately pulled his pants down to show me.

Sure enough, there was something between his legs that looked more male than female. He jumped up and down and wiggled it for me. So now I can write *him* in this notebook instead of *her*.

Yeah, I'm glad I don't have Lilo's empathy talent. I let the loki fill me up with cotton and had a go at him. After a few seconds of that I had to clutch the mattress to keep my balance. It was like being inside a bouncing ball, with colors and emotions and pain piercing me like—well, like sex. I guess that's how Lilo sees everything. Fortunately, he had vivid memories of the Lyrridog. I even caught some words, which I almost never do.

"—with the beautiful eyes—with the beautiful eyes—" The angel is leaning over Lilo and thrilling him with fear and desire, making him long for his own prolonged and exquisite death. "—the girl with the beautiful eyes, do you know her— with the beautiful eyes—"

"Shade! Shade! Shade! Shade! Shade!" is all Lilo can offer, because he's so swept away.

Stone was quite different. He was a dark pool, very cold and deep. Swimming there was like smothering in the amniotic fluid of a dead womb, but I had to go deeper to see the Lyrri clearly. No words this time, but an understanding between the two of them, and a desire that was like sex and death at the same time. I didn't stick around to sort out who the feeling belonged to, but got out of there as soon as I could. Then I sat back to rest.

Lilo started bouncing off the walls, and Stone called him back. Stone looked me in the eye, and I'll wager he didn't know I had read him. Maybe he thought we were playing "which one of us is tougher." Well, I know *he* is, and I don't give a shit.

Smoked all Ramona's loki and ate all the food I could get my hands on. Then I got up and walked to the door. On the way out, I leaned over Stone and said, "You've been selling it too long." He looked up and surprised me with a penetrating look, almost like he was scoping me back. Gave me a little twinge between the legs, though that might have been caused by the loki. Or the fact that I haven't had sex for a long time. Or maybe it was just that I had to work so hard to read him, I ended up getting more intimate than usual.

Anyway, I sure don't feel anything for him now. Thanks to him, I can't hang out at the Baby School anymore, not unless I want to run into that Lyrri-dog. One of my major food sources cut off.

I'll have to crash in the hidey-hole again. Maybe I'm gonna die, but I'm not gonna do it tonight!

I found the Salvation Army my first week on Z'taruh. I had been looking all over Capital for the Human/Earth Embassy. Nothing outside of Capital except swamp and marshes, so I didn't have far to look. But it turns out there's no embassy of any kind on Z'taruh. The closest I came to it is Z'taruhn Fauna Control; and they're not interested in anything with less than four feet.

I've forgotten a lot of stuff that happened in between, but I'll never forget that first week. The Salvation Army gave me my second good meal on this planet. But more important, that was the day I met the elephant man.

I had wondered how Skids survived. During the day they haunt Midtown and the Spacer Sector, hoping to bum enough money to buy booze or meltdown. But they didn't look like they were starving to death, and I was, so I decided to follow them and see where they were getting fed. I couldn't believe it when I saw the Salvation Army sign. Halfway across the galaxy from Earth, and I was standing in a chow line with a bunch of derelicts.

I was busy sniffing the odors drifting from the kitchen when I felt a presence behind me. I turned and looked up into an elephant's face.

He had to be ten feet tall and four feet wide. The elephant man. I mean, this being his tusks, and ears, and a trunk. Brown eyes stared back at me from deep folds of grey skin. He raised a three-fingered hand and pointed.

He said, "The line is moving."

I shut my mouth and ran to keep my place. I wanted to stare at him again, but I waited until we were inside and I had my stew. I hung back in the crowd and watched to see where he would sit. I expected the ground to shake as he walked past me and into the big dining room, but a butterfly would have made more noise. It was uncanny. He sat at a table near the back, facing so that he could see the entire room. I got my gall together and went to sit at the same table.

Two other derelicts were already there; one a Ragnir River Man, all green skin and fangs, with a face that was a cross between a crocodile and a frog. The other was a human bag lady; a big woman who I immediately pegged as the strong, silent type. They watched me curiously as I tried to get up the nerve to speak.

As I struggled, the room slowly filled. The big blowers kicked on overhead, making an ungodly racket, and cooler air began to push the hot air around. I sighed with relief, but I was the only one.

"My name is Shade," I finally blurted.

The elephant man didn't answer. He watched me as he ate his stew, his big hands moving with incredible grace. Spoonful after spoonful disappeared behind that trunk as old brown eyes summed me up. I felt like a buffoon.

But then he said, "I am Knossos."

I thought it was a wonderful name. I'm glad I already had my shades back then, because my eyes must have been really wide.

I was so flustered when he actually told me his name that it took me several more minutes to speak again. In the meantime, a lion man and a wolf man came to sit at our table. They nodded respectfully to Knossos, whose returning nod was quietly gracious. He finished eating, put his bowl aside, and folded his massive hands on the table.

"You've never seen an elephant man before?" he asked me.

"Not up close," I said. "I mean not to talk to. I've seen Aesopians in vids, but you're much better in person!"

That was so dumb, so much like what a fan would say to a vid star, but Knossos just took it at face value.

"Yes," he said. "Images and recordings are poor replacements for reality."

I glanced nervously at the lion man, whose reality I would much rather have forgone. I was attacked by a lion man my third day on Z'taruh because I had walked past him without acknowledging his presence. Lion men can be touchy that way. But this one seemed subdued. Still, it made me nervous to see his teeth scratching grooves into his spoon as he tried to maneuver it into that muzzle of his.

"Are you a Ragnir vet?" I asked Knossos.

"Yes. Many in this room are veterans from that war, and other wars as well."

Snag pointed his spoon at me. "Girl. I see you going through the trash near fast-food stalls, like Skid. How come you don't wrap yourself and hunt the tables? You too young to be here."

"I just want to eat," I said.

"There is no shame in that," Knossos said, though I have never seen him go through trash to eat. It would break my heart to see that.

"But rag-wraps be cooler!" Snag laughed, making sounds like a steaming tea kettle. "Much cooler than regular clothes. Perfect for Z'taruh climate." He laughed again, because, as usual, he was only wearing a loincloth.

"How come you're here now?" I asked Knossos.

His brown eyes were rock-steady on mine. Maybe he could see past the shades after all.

"We are here because we lost the war, and we must now do the best we can. Like you, little Shade."

The lion man and the wolf man stopped eating, and for a moment, the table was very quiet. Too quiet. In fact, I couldn't even hear the blower any more. The only sound was my heart beating. Knossos was sitting across from me, but he also seemed to be farther away; and instead of rags I saw metal and leather on his huge body. The wolf man and lion man wore space armor—Snag and Mira, too. They were younger, stronger; and Knossos, standing at their center, leading them into battle, was their king. Behind them, through the mist, was a wonderful city—

Knossos touched my shoulder. "Shade." His voice thrummed in my ears like a war drum. "Are you all right?"

I was sitting at the table again, and the blowers were making their usual racket.

"Fine," I said. "Just dizzy. I'm still getting used to the heat." I picked up my spoon, which I had dropped in my lap, and began to eat again.

Knossos considered me for a long moment. "You're a strange young woman," he said at last. But the way he said it, it sounded like a compliment, like he was saying there was more to me than there seemed to be. I smiled at him.

"What kind of world is—ah—do you call it Aesop?"

"No. We call it Home. But you may refer to *us* as Aesopians, as all do."

"So what is it like? Is it like Earth?"

"I have only seen vids of your Earth," said Knossos, "and I find them unreliable. Perhaps there are superficial similarities."

"Like what?" I persisted.

"Home is a world of great mountains and bottomless canyons. Huge fissures crack the earth, the scars of a war one hundred thousand years in the past. It is a world of ancient forests, mountainshaking storms, and cities that challenge the gods."

"Sounds pretty neat," I said.

I thought I saw one corner of his mouth appear from behind his trunk. "It is," he said.

"Huh," Snag interrupted. "Home rivers too cold and fast. And not enough mud."

I thought of the wonderful city I had glimpsed, and pictured Knossos walking through its streets. I screwed up my courage and scoped him; but his mind is so disciplined and his ego so strong, I really couldn't penetrate far. But what I felt was interesting. I got a clearer impression of the people around me, as Knossos sees them.

When I think back on it, that was probably the start of our partnership.

But I didn't go back to the Salvation Army for a long time after that. I was busy learning to be a Deadtowner. Snag is right—rag-wraps are cooler.

Eventually, I just had to go back and see Knossos again. When he saw me, he said, "I'm glad you came back. I would like to speak to your further on the subjects of war and history."

I've had a lot of meals at the S.A. since then, and when Knossos is here I eat with him. Tonight I'm sleeping here. Lilo and Stone won't know about that. No one asks—or answers—any dumb questions here.

Don't misunderstand. I didn't need their food or shelter before now. It was Knossos that kept me coming here. For the first time in my life, I could share a conversation that was more than skin deep. Skin is something Knossos has plenty of.

Scarbabies have skin too. Judas-goat skin. Cuts and burns and bruises to the bone.

Maybe it's because I'm so tired, but I can't seem to hate them right now.

Back on Earth I thought I knew everything. Fourteen years old, and I had it figured out. By then I was taking care of myself and Katie, who was ten. I fed us, did the shopping, made all the doctor appointments. We weren't fighting much anymore. I even tried to handle the finances, but Mom didn't like that. She was afraid the whole house of cards would come down if anyone breathed on it.

I thought we were poor, too. We ate a lot of hamburger and chicken, couldn't afford the fancy ice cream. We lived in one of the nicest condos in Hollywood, but when school started in the fall I didn't have new clothes.

God, I hated that. I had miserable taste in clothes, but I loved them.

I was hefty, too, though you wouldn't believe it if you saw me now. I had zits all over my face (that's mostly cleared up, too). Before I had my eyes done, I could have worn a paper bag over my head and no one would have minded. Including me.

So I was in a peculiar situation, because we lived in a rich neighborhood and went to a snobby school (I was an A student); my mom was a society freak, invited to all the parties, dozens of classical albums to her credit. And we ate hamburger.

The kids I knew were almost as mean as Deadtowners. Guess all that money rots your brain.

Mom tried to do special things for us, in between the times she wasn't contemplating permanent flight. When I look back I realise that our stomachs were full, our beds warm, and we always had Christmases and birthdays. For my fifteenth birthday, Mom bought me sculpted eyes.

"It's just some minor surgery, electrolysis, and—I don't know—some kind of chemical treatment to permanently tint your lids," she said when she was trying to talk me into it.

"But it costs an arm and a leg!" I said.

"You're worth it. You're my beautiful daughter, and you deserve it."

She was the only person on Earth who thought I was beautiful. I decided I'd better humor her.

So we headed on down to the Body Sculpting Plaza. I'd been there once before with Mom, when she had her neck done. I was feeling okay as we walked up to the main entrance, but when we got inside where the displays and offices and waiting rooms were, all crowded with anxious and nervous women, I was beginning to feel a bit twitchy.

"How about if we get Shade some boobs, too?" said Katie.

"You're going to need a new nose in a minute," I told her. But the distraction had made me feel a little better.

We went into Doctor Garcia's office and signed in. He was the same guy who did Mom's neck. I think he must have had a thing for her, because he came out immediately and ushered us into the prep room, ignoring three customers who had already been waiting there awhile.

I sat down at a display console and watched Mom pick out some eyes for me. "Is this going to hurt?" I kept asking the doctor.

"Of course not," he said. "You'll be out of here in under two hours."

Actually, it seemed even shorter than that, because after he put me under, I was completely unconscious. It felt like two minutes had passed. I woke up with bandages over my eyes.

"When can I take these things off?" I asked Mom as she ushered me back to the train.

"In the morning," she promised. So I spent the rest of the day being bored to death.

In the morning I got up and immediately tore the stuff off my upper face. I went to look at myself in my bathroom mirror.

I had to laugh. The eyes were beautiful, all right. They looked like they had been stolen from an Italian Madonna and plastered on my poor face.

"Everything okay in there?" my mom called through the door.

I let her in.

"They're gorgeous!" She cradled my face in her hands and beamed.

"I love them," I lied. I didn't add that I thought I could use a whole new body to go with them.

"Good," she said. "Now you can go out and get a job. Unless you want to live somewhere else, that is."

Feeling hot. Had the best day I've had in a long time. Got up early and re-wrapped myself, so I was nice and tight and ready for action. I skipped the free breakfast at the S.A. I wanted to see if I could earn it myself at the fast-food stalls.

I did good. Made a real nuisance of myself with the tinkers and government workers, most of whom have been around long enough to know better. I burned it off almost as soon as I ate it, but that's okay. I was more like my old self.

So I just couldn't resist hopping a transport to the pits to check out the fighters. I almost never go there by myself. The Q'rin don't like humans in their part of town, especially Deadtowners. But what the hell, I'm a reckless gal.

It was funny to watch the faces of the people who got on as I rode through the Spacer Sector. Some of them stared at me like I was an exotic animal. Others watched me warily; but it didn't do them much good. I lifted almost enough to buy myself a ticket to the fights. Then I sat back and enjoyed the view of the wonderful, glitzy Spacer Sector, with its casinos and hotels and shops. We rode right through its center for about forty-five minutes until the fortified walls and fortress-like buildings of the Q'rin sector came into view. Most of the humans had gotten off the train by then. Only a few of us pit-fans were left.

My heart leapt as the colosseum and outbuildings of the pits came into view. I almost felt like going in and trying my luck; and if I had brought some muscle to protect my earnings, I might have done that. But for the time being I decided just to scope the outskirts, for future reference.

I got out at the muddy field just outside the main complex. Q'rin-dogs roamed all over the place. Seems like there are more dogs in Capital every day. I hate them, the way they strut around like they own everything. We don't have a police force on this planet. We have rich people who have standing armies of mercenaries.

I have to admit the Q'rin-dogs don't strut as much as the human ones do, maybe because they're bigger and tougher and don't have to prove as much. The Q'rin aren't pretty—they look kind of like oversized Neanderthals—but I think they have the nicest asses around, and I saw plenty of prime examples as I cruised the crowd, slipping in and out like the shade I was named for.

Lots of fighters hang out in the chow lines and the shanty bars in the field behind the pits, so that's where I went. Circled around and behind, dodging dogs and other creeps. Once there I got

an interesting surprise. There was an animal carnival in the field across from the shanties. I
think they call that field Packrat's Plot. So the
place was twice as crowded as usual. Lots of
human- and Lyrri-dogs as well as the Q'rin, and
a lot of Deadtowners. That's a combination that
spells pandemonium. I couldn't resist it.

Headed for the Sleaze Pit first. (That's not
really its name—none of the shanties have names.
They're just cheap pre-fab structures with holes
in the walls and a permanent stench.) That's
where some of the best fighters hang out, the
Lectrowhippers and the Manglers. Slipped in behind some tinkers and let the smells and sounds
curl around me.

I waited for the server to approach me, but he
never did. Couldn't figure out what was up. I
needed that drink to hide behind while I scoped
the joint. So, *okay,* I thought, *hit and run.* I would
scope until they chased me out.

So there I was, sitting behind my shades and
scoping like crazy—and I was getting lots of good
stuff—but something else was happening too. People were checking me out like I was a prostitute.
Especially this one Q'rin-dog a couple of tables
away. Couldn't figure it out. Everyone hates
Deadtowners; I mean, we even hate *each other.*
Other Deadtowners were getting the same attention, and they weren't fighting it off. It made me
mad, until I figured out what was going on.

They were hookers, dressed up like Deadtowners.
What a scream! I guess some people like to fuck
what they hate. Here were these hookers with
hacked-off hair and rag strips wrapped around
their bodies. Their plasti-fix jackets were really
made of vinyl. And they looked convincing I guess,

though I'm ashamed of myself for not scoping it right off. That's what happens when I take things for granted.

So this Q'rin-dog is checking me out like I'm one of them. I kept an eye on him and the scope on everyone else. Finally he comes over and says, "How much?"

I looked him up and down, wondering how long it would take him to figure it out. He was a big specimen, even bigger than most Q'rin, and young.

"How do you get one of those damned servers to come over and take an order?" I asked him. He raised a finger and instantly a server was at his side.

"What do you want?" the Q'rin asked me.

"Whiskey."

He nodded to the server, who rushed off. "You didn't answer my question," the Q'rin said. "How much are you."

"I think we've had a misunderstanding," I said. "I'm the real thing. That's supposed to mean you don't bother asking me to sell my ass. Because the answer is always no."

He seemed to get a kick out of that. "I knew you were a real Deadtowner." He sat down and showed me his teeth. "I've been on this mudball long enough to know the difference."

The drink came back with the server and the Q'rin paid him. I didn't say no. I wasn't done scoping yet, and I was a little curious too. He handed the drink to me.

"Whiskey isn't bad," he said. "Not as good as one of our Brainbusters, but not bad." He was looking at my meager breasts as he said this. I had to laugh. He wasn't bad either. He managed to make that rocky Q'rin face move in interesting ways. I pretended to sip the whiskey (I never drink, except with Knossos—rather have a smoke of loki any day) and continued to scope. I was learning a lot. I was almost tempted to ask him if he was a betting man.

Then an elephant man walked through the door and my heart stopped.

But it wasn't Knossos. This one was younger, and he was with a bear man.

"Do Aesopians frighten you?" The Q'rin nodded toward the elephant man. Guess my face must've gone white.

"No," I said. "How about you?"

The crack got to him, but not the way I thought it would. His smile just widened.

"We Q'rin won that war," he said. "The Aesopians lost. And you humans just went home. Since then we have found Aesopians better company than humans. Except for you, of course. What is your name?"

"Katie," I lied.

"I am Donokh."

"Mmmmm." I was almost done scoping. Some of the Lectrowhippers were proving difficult, so maybe I wasn't paying as much attention to Donokh as I should have. So when he reached over and whipped my shades off, I wasn't prepared.

I sat there for a moment with my mouth open and my sculpted eyes wide. I could tell he liked the eyes. He especially liked them on the face of a street urchin.

"I'll give you fifty credits," he said.

I was flattered. From what I hear, the going rate around here is twenty-five.

"Give 'em back," I said.

"I'm not done looking," he said.

"Neither is everyone else in this fucking place. I wear those for a reason."

He frowned, then nodded. "I see what you mean." He handed them back, and I settled them into place.

"You could make more if you showed your eyes," he said.

"I told you I'm a *Deadtowner*. If those broads wander too close to Deadtown with those vinyl jackets on they'll be sorry."

"In that case I have a duty to arrest you."

"What the hell are you hustling me for, pervert?"

"You could use a bath," he said, "but you shouldn't underestimate yourself. Drink your whiskey."

He watched me while I pretended to take another sip.

"So Donokh," I said, "how long have you been a dog?"

"Long enough," he said. "You shave the sides of your head like a pit fighter. Do you bet?"

I shrugged and looked at him sideways. "You?"

"Occasionally," he said.

Right. As we both sit there and check out the fighters.

"You ever win?" I asked him.

"Not as much as I would like to."

I scoped him as he said that. He wouldn't have been a bad betting partner if he hadn't been so interested in jumping my bones. Not that I don't like a little of that stuff sometimes. But not on the first night. Too easy to get fucked over that way.

Besides, I've been through some of those Q'rin raids at the Baby School. They even raid Deadtown

from time to time. The Q'rin are capable of a
degree of violence that human-dogs can't even
begin to match. And they're not as subtle as the
Lyrri. And Donokh seemed to like the fact that
I'm a Deadtowner a little too much. Maybe he
was planning to slap me around a little.

"You like animals?" I asked him.

"You mean the animal carnival?" He leaned
closer. "Maybe. I know a better place. Across the
field, a little closer to the pits. We can get
Brainbuster there."

I knew the place he meant. It would give me a
chance to check out some of the Q'rin fighters.

"Sounds good," I agreed.

We left the untouched whiskey on the table. It
was funny the way he took my arm and escorted
me out of there, smelly, grimy Deadtowner that I
am. Not that I don't wash my neck at the S.A.
from time to time.

But he was proud to have me with him as we
walked across the field, even though other Q'rin
gave us dirty looks. Guess I kind of liked that.

We sauntered into this other place, and it was
about ninety percent full of Q'rin men. A few
Aesopians here and there—Donokh is right about
them. I've always been surprised that Knossos
tolerated me, considering how my people backed
out on his. But it's always amazed me that Q'rin
and Aesopian warriors seem to like each other's
company so much considering what bitter enemies they were once.

But the most interesting thing about this joint
was that there were Q'rin courtesans in there.
Not hookers—fancy ladies. They stared at me
when I came in with Donokh, and I felt myself
being thoroughly examined. I returned the favor,

because I've never seen a Q'rin woman before who wasn't a fighter. These ladies were obviously in the company of specific men; and they had a beauty that, though not of the human sort, was intriguing.

Even the female fighters were sitting with men, and I was beginning to wonder if Donokh was possessive too.

All the servers were non-Q'rin, of course. Donokh snapped his fingers at one, and the server hurried over. He said something in Q'rin that probably translated to: "Bring us two Brainbusters."

I didn't care. I wasn't going to drink it no matter what it was.

"I've seen you around before," said Donokh, "with an Aesopian elephant man."

I didn't say yes or no.

"I admit that was one of the reasons I was curious to talk to you," he continued. "The elephant men are the highest noblemen of their society. They do not associate casually with lesser people."

That was news to me, but it didn't surprise me. Anyone can see Knossos should be a king, even through the rags he wears.

"Maybe hard times makes you lower your standards," I said. It was his turn not to answer. His face got kind of still and unreadable, and it occurred to me that he might have thought I was talking about him. I mean, his chasing after my flea-bitten self. Maybe he thought he was more interested in finding out about the elephant man, but if he did he was kidding himself.

"I would like to meet the elephant man," Donokh said. "I'll make it worth your while."

"Haven't seen him lately," I said.

He put fifty credits on the table. "Are you sure?"

"Positive. I haven't seen him since the last time we bet together."

He put another fifty down. "We have reason to believe he is forming a small army. As you know, Aesopians are not permitted to do that in this sector."

The army part surprised me. I know Knossos is a Ragnir veteran, but I didn't know he had been a high-ranking officer.

"I bet with him sometimes," I said. "I've eaten supper from the same chow line. That's it. Can't help you."

He put down fifty more credits, but kept his hand on the pile. "I'm sure you can remember more than that. A Deadtowner can use one hundred and fifty credits. If the money does not interest you, I can take you back to headquarters and we can help you remember there."

"Why ruin a nice evening?" I said. I didn't take the money. I scoped him. He was big, but it looked like he was probably fast enough to stop me before I reached the door.

"So if all you wanted to do was talk about Knossos, how come you tried to buy my ass?" I asked.

That got him. I think the fact that he was attracted to me was a little hard for him to handle. It's the sort of thing that makes a man take a good look at his values. But the feeling was there, and I took advantage of it.

"Look, I've told you as much as I can remember. I have a hard enough time worrying about myself to cover for anyone else, you know? Maybe later in the evening I'll remember something useful."

"Maybe," he agreed, properly diverted. He put a hand on my knee. "I know a good bath house."

I laughed. "Why wash it when it's just going to get dirty again?"

He thought that was funny. His hand started to radiate heat.

"Seriously," I said. "Let's check out the animal show. Be nice to walk around. I love animals." Besides, I had scoped this place for all it was worth.

"All right," he said, "If that's what pleases you." But his expression said, "The things you have to do to get laid!"

The sign over the gate said SHOW OF SHOWS! It also said LIMITED ENGAGEMENT, which usually means "We'll stay until we can't milk any more money out of you." The smell of too many animals was enough to make even a Deadtowner gag. I smiled at Donokh like I thought we were walking into the fanciest club in the Spacer Sector. He grinned back like he was really enjoying himself. I felt a pang of guilt, but I kept smiling.

I have to admit I was interested in the show despite myself. It was almost like a circus, sort of a zoo side-show—animals in cages and tanks, on perches or leashes or force fields. Performing animals and animals that were just there to look at.

And the audience was at least as interesting as the show, especially since there were so many Lyrri hanging around. I could have sworn I caught a glimpse of that Lyrri-dog from the other day over by one of the big-cat cages. When I looked again he was gone. Sent a shiver up my spine.

Donokh misread the action and put his arm around me.

"They're in cages," he said. "They can't hurt you."

"Yeah," I said. "I was just a little nervous about the crowd. Too many people."

"I thought Deadtowners liked crowds. All those pockets."

I gave him a mocking grin but didn't answer. I was too busy scoping the crowd for that glimpse of the predator. I felt *something*. Something that didn't come too close.

And in the meantime, I had this Q'rin-dog to deal with. So I walked around with him and waited for my chance.

The scorpion woman gave it to me.

She was Q'rin. Not a fighter, but maybe just as dangerous. She had an entire display area all to herself. Rainbow-colored scorpions ran up and down her body and around her feet. Some of them were so tiny they were just flashes of color. One big grey fellow was as long as my forearm and had *two* tails. She just stood there with her feet planted and her hands on her hips, watching the crowd with intense eyes.

I glanced at Donokh. He wore what looked like an expression of respect on his rocky face. He was enthralled, like the rest of the crowd. His arm was still around my waist.

Suddenly the scorpion woman flicked her hand, sending a big red scorpion after some human woman standing at the front of the crowd. The woman yelped and jumped, coming down on the foot of an Aesopian lion man. The Aesopian growled and went after her. The crowd surged forward.

Donokh was straining to get a look at what was happening. He let go of me. I let five or six people push between us before I yelled "Donokh!" and waved my arms like I was trying to get back to him. He turned and changed direction toward me. But he was swimming against the current. I just let more and more people get between us, and when I was out of sight behind more bodies, I turned and ran for all I was worth.

I thought one of the Lyrri-dogs lounging at the gate smiled at me as I ran past, but I was probably imagining it.

Now I'm in my hidey-hole, scribbling like mad under a beam of light from a crack in the shutters. My butt's falling asleep. In a moment I'll stretch out as far as I can in here and join it. I was just thinking. Maybe Knossos had a good reason for disappearing. Maybe he *is* putting an army together. He's the one who could do it. Maybe he's even got a ship.

Maybe I can get him to take me with him.

I got my first job back on Earth after my fifteenth birthday. Mom hadn't been kidding when she said I better get one or else. She stopped buying us groceries after the first week.

I couldn't even put her off with school. I had already graduated. We had one of those work-at-your-own-pace programs at Hollywood High. A moron could have zipped through that program. I dragged it out as long as I could, but I was still out before I was fifteen.

The first place I scored was a fast-food joint called Squeezie Freez. I had been eating there since I was nine, so I figured they owed me something. I went down in the morning to fill out an application.

"You want what?!" said the girl behind the counter, as if I had just asked her to give me all the money in the register.

"An application. Got one handy?"

"You know," she said as she fished behind the counter, "we aren't allowed to eat on the job."

Took her twenty minutes to find the application. Then she stared at me and whispered with the other girls while I filled it out. I ignored them.

"I'll give it to the manager when she comes in," she said when I handed the application back to her. I wasn't sure whether she would or not, but I figured it was all just part of the job-hunting game. I thanked her and went home.

I was surprised when the owner called me the next day and told me to come down. I wasn't entirely happy about it.

"Maybe you'll be able to get doodle bars at a discount," Katie offered. I think she was trying to cheer me up.

I walked into the owner's office and found her viewing one of those old *War Lust* pulps. On the screen, some "Q'rin warriors" were ravishing a beautiful human nurse. The owner, a dumpy woman in her late middle age, did not seem pleased to be interrupted. She looked up at me and said, "Uh oh, I don't think you and me are gonna get along."

Then she hired me to prove it.

I don't remember what I said to get the job because as I recall, I didn't want it all that much. So I couldn't have tried very hard. Maybe it was the fact that I was willing to work below minimum wage.

"See, businesses that net less than one hundred thousand a year aren't required to pay underage workers an adult wage," she said.

"Okay," I said.

"I'll give you a try then. And call me Agnes."

"Okay."

"We'll get you started taking orders. Follow me."

"Okay."

I was a nervous wreck that first day, because Agnes haunted my back constantly. Her way of teaching you how to do things was to scold you for doing them wrong.

"That's too much ice cream! They don't need a bag for that, it's already wrapped up! The deluxe burger only gets *one* pickle! Get your big butt out of the way! Don't put so many damn french fries in the bag! What, you think I'm rich?"

Finally, she drove off in the biggest, reddest *Chariot 666* I've ever seen, and everybody relaxed.

"Gee, she's kind of hyper, isn't she?" said Alison. She had been hired just three days before, and she was the only nice girl there.

Mom responded to the news of my job by taking me out and buying me some new outfits. "For work!" she said. "You'll have to look like a professional."

I picked everything out, so of course the clothes were absolutely atrocious. Agnes rolled her eyes when she saw them. Alison told me I looked nice.

On the third day, I discovered that automation could be a nightmare. I swear, I managed to screw up every machine in the joint. First, the shake machine.

"I think you need to push the cup all the way up to the top," Alison said, as the two of us mopped chocolate off the walls and ourselves. I let her make the next one.

Next, the burger machine. I had been doing all right with this one for the last few days, so I felt confident when a customer ordered two Deluxes and two BBQs, hold the onions. But I forgot to turn the BBQ button to *off* before I opened the serving door.

"Well, you've probably had your bad luck for the day," said Alison, as we mopped the mess off the floor.

And maybe she would have been right about that, if Agnes hadn't decided to pay us a surprise visit in the afternoon.

"How are you girls getting along by yourselves?" she asked us.

"Fine," we lied.

And everything was fine, until a customer came in about five minutes before Agnes was going to leave.

"I'd like a raspberry and chocolate dip cone with glow sprinkles," he said. "Make that a large."

I cringed. Alison was busy with the shake machine, and I was terrified of the dip machine.

"Go on, what are you waiting for?" Agnes snarled at me.

I made the cone all right, but when I turned it up-side down in the dip mixture, the ice cream fell out. Frantically, I fished it out with the stirring spoon.

"What the hell do you think you're doing?" said Agnes.

I glooped the ice cream back into the cone and tried to roll it in the glow sprinkles. It fell out again. The customer started to laugh.

"What the hell do you think you're doing!" Agnes yelled.

"Hey, leave her alone," the customer said. "Just put it in a dish, kid. I'll eat it that way."

He left happy, and Agnes left without saying anything to me.

"Maybe she'll have forgotten about it by tomorrow," said Alison.

But the next day, Agnes called me at home as I was about to leave for work. "Don't bother coming in," she said. "I hired a new girl today, and she's working out fine. I'll mail you your check."

"Okay," I said.

See how easy that was?

I tried the housekeeping racket next. Got the idea from our own housekeeper.

"Hey, I have to turn people down!" she told me. "I've got a waiting list as long as my arm."

"Yeah," I said, "but can you make a living at it?"

"I've got three kids and no husband. But my condo is bigger than yours, I have a new tran, and we definitely eat better than you." She poked me in the chest.

"Let's see that list."

So I started to clean the houses of rich people. I was nervous as I went to the first house, sure that I would have an experience like at Squeezie Freez. But when Mrs. Zuckerman opened the door, she gave me a big hug.

"I'm so glad to see you!" she said.

"You are?"

"Oh yes, darling, the place is a *mess!*" And she ushered me into her perfectly spotless home.

The place had stain-free rugs with automatic vacuum sprites, bathroom fixtures that came clean with one rinse, and was a dust-free environment. I literally had nothing to do all day except answer the phone and fold towels. I didn't even have much laundry to do, because they had those newfangled disposable clothes, and a laundry service for the sheets. After six hours of this, I expected her to tell me she didn't need me after all. But instead, she hugged me again.

"Thank God you came!" she said. "See you in two days?" And she gave me a fat tip. She was already paying me three times the minimum wage, so I didn't know what to say about the extra money.

"Okay," I finally blurted out.

Within a week, my schedule was full of clients just like Mrs. Zuckerman. I kept most of them as regulars for almost a year. I ended up earning ten times what I had earned at Squeezie Freez. But the money was not as important as what I learned from those jobs.

I'm not talking about how I learned to look busy while doing nothing, or how status is more important to people than good work. I already knew those things. I'm talking about scoping.

"She has such an uncanny sense about people!" Mom used to tell people. "When she doesn't like someone, I stay away from them." And she usually did.

I don't remember exactly when I started getting feelings about people that turned out to be true. Maybe I always had them. Growing up in Hollywood tends to hone your senses, and work-

ing in the homes of the biggest movers and shak-
ers in town was quite an education.

I found myself wondering, *What makes them so
great?* Like Mr. Landry, who could hardly put a
sentence together.

"I got no respect for people who can't get no
sense, irregardless," he used to tell me. I still
have no idea what that was supposed to mean.

"Okay," I always said.

But Mr. Landry had more money than anyone,
and when people crossed him, they disappeared—or
changed their minds real fast. He worried and
intrigued me. Once, when I was following him
down the stairs to his basement, I started wondering real hard about him, actually concentrat-
ing on him. I guess I must have been a little
nervous about going down there alone with him.

His body blurred and changed into this thing
that looked like a shark would if it had arms and
legs. It moved down those stairs with a big grin
on its face, and I got this feeling from it like
what a snake might feel as it's about to put the
bite on a mouse. The thing started to turn its
head to look at me, and I screamed.

Mr. Landry almost fell the rest of the way
down the stairs. "What?!" he demanded, clutching his heart. "What the hell is it?!"

I was backing up the stairs by then. "Um—
ah—I saw a rat!"

"No way! There's not a rat within miles of
this place. My exterminator sees to that."

"I saw one," I insisted. "I can't go down there."

So from then on, he didn't try to make me go
down in the basement. He was pretty understanding about it, which is funny. I learned a lot
more about him after that, and about my other

clients. I learned what made them different from me and other ordinary people.

Mr. Landry was different because he thought he was. Mrs. Zuckerman was different because she was in the right place at the right time. You tell me which is more important.

I milked some extra money out of my clients once I knew everything there was to know about them. Except for Mr. Landry, who would have put me in a basket if I had tried to bleed him. What I earned helped put us in the black, and even bought some neat clothes for Katie and me.

Still, all good things must come to an end, sometimes with something that seems even better. My mom got a tour gig in Europe.

"I can't take you with me, but I'll be sending money home every month for food and rent and everything you'll need. You'll have to take care of Katie and the house, dear, and of course you'll have to quit your job, and—" Blah, blah, blah, blah, etc.

Mom hadn't packed her big bags in over a year, so I half-believed her about how everything was going to be all right. She took us to our favorite clothing shops and bought everything in sight.

"We'll have a tailor fix those so they fit you properly, dear," she said tactfully as she eyed my chubby body.

Katie, who normally didn't sense trouble in Mom, kept tugging my arm and whispering, "Is it really true?"

"I don't know," was all I could tell her. Mom was happier than I'd ever seen her, and she was usually depressed when she was thinking of running away. I was confused.

"I promise to send you tickets to Paris for my

grand finale," she told us. Then she took me aside and whispered, "Promise me you'll lose weight by then, sweetheart. Then I'll take you shopping in Paris."

"Okay, Mom. I promise."

She took the big bags down from the attic and packed them. I stood by, my hands itching. "Isn't this exciting!" she kept gushing.

"You bet, Mom," I said.

The checks came on time for the first few months. Then a couple of them came late. Then they stopped altogether. The end of the tour came and went, but Mom never sent for us. And she never came home.

Finally, I took Katie to stay with our aunt by the same name. I didn't want to admit to them what was really going on. I didn't want to ruin their perfect image of Mom, like mine had been ruined long ago. I stayed for awhile myself, but I couldn't feel welcome. I wanted to run away from Mom like she had run away from me.

So I took the first step on my long journey to Z'taruh. I went down to Spaceport California to find a job.

Shade.
I have discovered your notebook. As you can see, I know where your hidey-hole is. Meet me tonight at the front gate of the animal show. I will not hurt you. I want to talk about business.

Chaz the Lyrri.

It's actually cold here. Wind is coming through the holes left by plundered plasti-fix, the same stuff I'm wearing for a jacket. What's left is blowing around, making scary shadows jump all over the room. I can't sleep. Maybe I won't sleep until it's day again. Though in Deadtown, day isn't any safer than night.

Don't know what I'm going to do.

I walked into my hidey-hole and read my journal for fifteen minutes before I found the note. I wonder if Chaz was watching me then. I bet he was.

It took every scrap of talent I had to scope my way out of Midtown without being followed. I'm hungry. This really stinks. When I look out the window, all I see is rotting skeletons where buildings used to be. Feel like I'm miles up. The bugs don't even fly this far up. I can see the whole mess. Deadtown makes Midtown look brand new.

I haven't gone this far into Deadtown for months. Because of Knossos. I wanted to be closer to his side of town. I'm not sure I've still got contacts in here.

Well, maybe one. Blackie. She'll take anyone in. But it's no free ride. One night with Blackie can make you feel ten years older.

Last time I saw her, I called her a rich bitch and told her if she died tomorrow the worlds would grind on past without even glancing down. I knew what that would do to her. It's kind of sad that I still don't care.

So what's to lose? I'll bet she'll act like nothing ever happened. Flaky. But it's better than sitting here jumping at shadows.

Maybe.

I went straight to Blackie's building, even though it was the middle of the night. To her that's like afternoon. She doesn't wake up until the sun is on its way down.

Of course there was a party going on—about twenty Deadtowners drinking and smoking and squawking and stinking. Blackie's voice kept rising above everyone else's. Same old shit. I slipped past the lookouts and up the stairs to the comfortable suite on the fifth floor. Blackie lives in one of the few intact buildings in Deadtown, with her drugs and her dresses and her fair-weather friends. I was sitting on her couch eating junk food for at least twenty minutes before she noticed me.

For one awful moment she was wide open and I read all of the fear and confusion she felt at my sudden appearance. Then that famous Blackie static flooded the room three times stronger than usual. I could feel my skin aging in the radiation.

"I can't believe it!" she gushed. "It's the ultimate Deadtowner!"

I didn't answer, just shoved a handful of Potato Peps into my mouth. Silence is the best way to put Blackie in her place. I couldn't scope her with all that static she was throwing out, but the look on her face said, "I knew you'd be back!" Other than that, her hair is black again and she's plumper than usual. She was wearing one of her gypsy dresses and the high-top walking shoes she was so proud of. Her olive skin was freshly scrubbed, and her nails, as usual, were painted black.

"Who invited you?" asked Jake. I was interested to see he was still hanging on.

"Oh, you're just jealous because Shade is prettier than you," Blackie said, knowing it was true.

"You're looking good," I said to Blackie. "Things must be going well."

She gave me her famous enigmatic smile, and

it really made her face look beautiful. But long ago I learned that her smile is like a fan that Blackie opens to conceal herself.

"How come you haven't come to see me?" she asked.

"How come you haven't come to see me?" I repeated. It's scary how quickly we fell into the old patterns. "I've been taking care of myself," I quickly added. "Now I'm here to see you."

"Lucky us," Jake said. Jake is a smart Deadtowner, but a stupid lover. He moved into Blackie's suite a year ago and planted himself like a red-headed weed. Now he thinks he owns it and Blackie. He thinks his living here is going to make it harder for Blackie to fool around. After a year he still doesn't realise how much she loves to push his buttons.

"How long can you stay?" asked Blackie.

"A few weeks."

I polished off the Potato Peps and waited. This was the point where she was supposed to tell me how long I could really stay. But she didn't say anything. It was weird.

I poked the kid next to me, who was so new to Deadtown that his rag-wraps were sagging around his ankles. (No one shows you how to do the wraps, you have to figure it out on your own.)

"Got any loki?" I asked.

He didn't look at me. "Ask *her*," he said softly.

Blackie was already going to fetch the stash box. She put it down in front of me, and insisted on sitting between me and the new kid. She lit one and slipped it between my lips, just like Ramona likes to do. She would be really mad if I ever told her that. She put her arm around the back of the couch and crossed her legs, looking at me and hiding behind the smile. I hoped she couldn't see this notebook under my wraps. If she knew about it, she'd want to read it.

"You're looking skinny and sexy, as usual," she said.

"I'm starving. What else have you got to eat?"

"Lots of junk. You should eat it before I do. I'm so fat."

"Only for a Deadtowner," I said. "Everyone else would think you were normal."

That was the wrong thing to say. The smile intensified.

"I know I'm not a Deadtowner. I just hang out with you guys. I don't even have that sexy haircut." She ran her hand over my head just a little more roughly than she had to, and then yanked at her own, shoulder-length hair.

"Don't start with that crap again." Jake threw an empty Cheez Chip box at her. She deflected it.

"It's true!" she said. She put her other arm around the new kid and bumped him with her boobs. "Even Farouk here is Dead-er than I am, aren't you Farouk?"

Farouk gave her a stiff shrug, carefully avoiding her eyes. He looked like he was sure she would throw him out any minute.

"Isn't he cute?" Blackie pressed herself against Farouk again, and his brown skin took on a reddish color. "Don't you just want to fuck his brains out?"

"No," Jake said resentfully, "but you do."

Blackie pouted at him. She took her arm away from Farouk. "Don't hate me," she whispered. He just glared at her. The two of them really seemed to be getting into it. I wanted to puke up my Potato Peps.

Everyone else had already grown bored with the exchange and had started new shouting matches, fights, feel-up contests, and expeditions to the kitchen for more food. I joined in with the last group, taking the loki with me and leaving Blackie and Jake with poor Farouk.

I had these friends back in Hollywood—Jackie and Cheryl B. They had conned their rich parents into letting them have their own apartment. Their kitchen was stocked pretty much like Blackie's, and it was almost as messy. Tons of food—fancy and junky. Lots of alcohol and drugs. And it was filled with dopey knick-knacks, the kind only young girls or little old ladies like to collect, scattered all over without any rhyme or reason.

Deadtowners knocked Blackie's knick-knacks over or threw them at each other as they plundered her kitchen. That won't matter to Blackie. She'll just steal more, probably from her own rich family. I found a corner to eat my spoils. I pushed aside a little moo-cow creamer that reminded me of one Mom used to have.

Everyone went to their own corners, as far away as they could get from each other, even the ones who had been feeling each other up in the other room. Eating is serious business. The unwashed Deadtowner smell in that little room could have killed a moose.

"So, Shade," one guy said around a mouthful, "been a long time. I hear you been taking your meals with Skids and Babies."

I gave him the onceover. Easier to scope out of Blackie's range. He started to twitch after a moment. "I don't know you," I said finally. Which was true. Didn't waste any more time on him.

A couple of the others snickered at him, but I could feel the hostility leaning toward me. Deadtowners pride themselves on their independent natures, but they really do have a strict code. Just because I fit in better with them than I ever have with anyone else doesn't mean I fit in.

Thumps and shrieks from Blackie in the other room echoed into the kitchen. After a moment Farouk wandered in looking truly disgusted and alone. I scoped him idly. He might make a good Deadtowner if he could break away from Blackie's "protection." Right now, he's more of a Runaway than anything else.

He got his food without any trouble from anyone, but he wouldn't have lasted a second if there hadn't been plenty to go around. He cringed when Blackie came in, but she had forgotten him already.

She started to pull dozens of different kinds of alcohol out of the cupboards. She had enough there for a wedding. She dumped some of it in a big bowl. It was Blackie's Special, and a definite indication that she planned to be knocked out for the next few days.

"I want you guys to help me drink this," she said.

I knew that things were about to get a lot weirder and wilder than I liked, so I got up to go find a hole to sleep in. But I wasn't getting off that easy.

"Shade!" she screeched. "Where the hell are you going?"

I didn't answer.

"Aren't you even going to give me a decent hello?" she said.

I didn't move.

She hugged me and kissed me on the mouth.
Then she went happily back to her mixing bowl.
If I had moved even a muscle, she would have
stuck her tongue down my throat. But now, as
usual, she knew I wasn't interested. So there
would be no more tests of that nature for a while.

Blackie pulled the cork out of a bottle with
Q'rin writing on it and mixed it with a quart of
vodka in the bowl. "Here are the rules," she said.
"I'm gonna pass this around, and everyone has to
have at least one shot glass of it. Then I'm gonna
pass it around again . . ."

I backed out the door and made my way up the
stairs. I had to climb to the eighth floor before I
found a quiet spot, a large bedroom suite with its
own bathroom. The bathroom still worked, including the shower, which I wasn't interested in
yet. Maybe later.

Farouk is asleep in the other bedroom. When
he came in earlier, he had been surprised to see
me and had almost backed out again.

"Don't leave on my account," I said.

"I'm not gonna fuck you," he said.

"You're damn right you're not," I said. "I don't
go for guys who haven't passed puberty yet."

Some kids might have been insulted by that,
but he seemed relieved. He came in, sat down,
pulled out some loki, and handed it to me. "Noticed you like this," he mumbled. He smoked a
little with me.

"I could fuck Blackie," he said, half-bragging.

"You want to?"

"Yeah."

Yeah. But the thought also scared him half to
death. It would scare me too, and I'm twice his age.

"Take some advice," I said. "Don't touch her."

He didn't answer that.

"You ever cruised the fast-food stalls?" I asked.

"Once or twice," he said. It was a lie.

"Tomorrow I'll show you how to do it," I said.

"What do I got to do for that?"

"Just don't snore tonight. And if your feet stink, point 'em in another direction."

He relaxed and nodded. "You finish this off. I'm going to sleep." And he did.

I can't sleep. I've been trying to convince myself I don't hate it here. Trying not to see the smug, satisfied look in Blackie's eyes now that I'm back. If I'm not careful, I could turn into something I can't stand, something other people laugh at.

Maybe I already have.

I spent my last few months on Earth scrounging for a way to get off-planet. I knew some people who worked for Security at Spaceport California, and they promised me I would have no trouble getting a job there. They were right. All they wanted was proof that I was over eighteen and assurance that I had never been convicted of a major crime. The latter was no problem, but the age thing had me scared. I was sure they would kick me out of their office as soon as they saw my fake I.D.

They lady who reviewed my application had a bored, cynical expression on her face. She barely glanced at my I.D. "When can you start?" she asked me.

"Tomorrow," I said.

"Not so fast. There are some things we have to get out of the way first."

Uh-oh, I thought. *This is it.*

But instead, she said to go to such-and-such an office downtown and get fingerprinted, fill out tax forms, attend a couple of classes on Spaceport security—

"—and you're in, kid. Get to it."

So I got my fingers inked, made up a bunch of stuff for the forms, and reported for a class that consisted of one hour of vids on spaceport detection equipment in action.

"See that big black blotch?" my instructor asked me. "That's a force gun."

"Wow," I said. "Imagine trying to hide a force gun in an uncomfortable place like *that*."

"Now," she said. "Look at these scans here. See how this suitcase looks like a solid black mass? What should you do?"

"Examine it by hand."

"Correct. And what if nine bags in a row scan as solid black, and it's the rush hour, and passengers are screaming at you to hurry and threatening you."

"Check 'em all by hand."

"Correct. And what if a passenger continues to set off the radiation detector even after removing everything from his or her pockets, all jewelry, and his or her hat?"

"Strip search. In private, of course."

"And what if, once the clothing is removed and nothing strange is apparent, the detector is still set off? What do you do?"

"I look the other way while the police officer gets a rubber glove and a lightwand."

"Good girl."

I started that very day, and immediately began to unlearn most of the things I had just been taught. One truth prevails with spaceport security: turnover. People were always quitting. It paid minimum wage, the equipment was faulty, and the hours were long. It was boring. I could scope better than the machines could scan, and the only "weapons" I intercepted were some fireworks a ten-year-old kid was trying to smuggle in his luggage.

But I hung on, sharing an apartment with six other people, saving my money, and eating beans. I was keeping my eyes and ears open for the real work, the work only the coyotes could get me. The illegal work on the big freighters. Runaway heaven, supposedly.

After four months of security nonsense a coyote finally approached me in the snack bar. I had seen him before, but I was careful not to make eye contact. He edged closer and finally said:

"Can't believe how expensive these damn snack bars are."

"Only game in town," I answered.

"Slow, too. Bet you're already late for work."

"Yep."

"How do you like working for security?"

"It stinks."

I was terrified he would walk away. Coyotes are like that sometimes. Malicious and paranoid.

"Yeah, I heard it don't pay much," he said finally.

"You heard right. But I'm kind of new, you know? Just starting out. Waiting for something better to come along."

"Sometimes you have to take chances to get ahead."

"I'm ready for that."

He pulled out a cigarette and smoked it for a

while, even though that's against the rules in the snack bars. Maybe that explained the grungy smell he had on him.

"There are two kinds of workers in the space biz, kid. Union and non-union. Non-union is another word for illegal. Sometimes it's another word for dead. But the freighters are always looking for non-union workers. You know why?"

"Because they don't have to pay 'em as much."

"That's right. But that don't mean you can't make money if you're non-union. You can make plenty."

"Yeah, I bet you can make more than a security guard."

"About ten times more." He blew smoke in my face and looked me over. "So. I bet you're one of those kids who dreams about being a spacer."

"Well, you know. I'm sixteen. I think I'm old enough."

"Can't get a license at sixteen."

"I could pass for eighteen—"

"Yeah, well, I'll see you around," he said, and he was gone.

A lot of coyotes never come back after that first interview. Lots of narcs look even younger than I do. It's a dangerous biz.

But this coyote did come back.

He sat in the seat next to me at the snack bar again and said, "I bet your parents wouldn't want you to space out," like he was picking up the conversation exactly where he left off.

"They wouldn't if they were around," I said. "I haven't seen either of them for some time now."

"Lucky you," he said.

"Yeah. I get to make my own decisions. And I know what I want."

"That's good. Because once you get started on a certain path, it can be unhealthy to change your mind."

"I hear you."

"Good," he said. "See you around."

And he was gone again. But this time I knew he was coming back. So I kept going to that snack bar, and eventually he sat down with me again.

"You have to realize," he said, "that opportunities can come up real sudden. You have to be ready at all times to take them."

"Okay," I said, and that night I sold all my stuff to my roommates and gathered all the cold cash I could. I bought a money belt and carried it with me. The next day, the coyote came up to me while I was eating lunch.

"Meet me at loading bay F," he said, and walked away.

I waited ten minutes before I followed. I had been scanning the bay assignments for weeks, so I knew a deep space freighter called the *Aguirré* was docked there. I had been hoping for something like that. My heart was pounding. I was sure everyone was looking at me.

Loading bay F was at the other end of the spaceport, a good seven miles from where I was, so I hopped on the Intersystem Tran to get there. For all I know, the coyote was in the car next to mine. I hoped I wasn't following him too closely.

I watched the port complex blur past me and felt a twinge of regret. I could have stayed in Hollywood and gone back to the housekeeping thing. But my excitement at the prospect of going into deep space was a lot stronger. Even now I can't say I regret my decision to leave Earth. I got off the tran and rode up several lifts until I came to the mouth of loading bay F.

The *Aguirré* was at the far end, already hooked up to the massive transport that would take it out to the field. I was so overwhelmed by the sight of it, I didn't move for several minutes.

Since then I've seen more impressive ships; especially the war ships, both Q'rin and human, whose lines are so clean and deadly. They're built for speed and punch; freighters are built to last long and go far.

But the *Aguirré* was a beautiful sight as it sat in the cavernous loading bay, looking like some madman's cathedral from an alien religion. Its sensors and observation bubbles and other equipment looked like spires and turrets to me; and there were even some objects that, when looked at sideways, almost resembled gargoyles. A lot of that stuff has to be retracted for exit and re-entry through atmosphere, but I didn't know that then. So the only thing that really looked like part of a spaceship to me was the stardrive.

I thought I'd never seen anything so big. But there are bigger freighters around than the *Aguirré*. They just never come down into atmosphere.

Eventually I remembered the coyote, who had been trying to get my attention for some time. He was signaling me frantically. He wanted me to follow him into one of the locker rooms. I did, my mouth dry.

The locker room was empty, but he was still motioning me to follow him. Finally he opened a closet and pointed to a bundle of clothes on the floor.

"Put those on and give me your uniform," he said. "But first let's have the money."

I pulled out the money belt and handed it to him. He looked at it quickly to make sure it was full of the real thing, then shoved me into the closet.

I put on the T-shirt and shorts that lay on top of the bundle, then a janitor's uniform and some work shoes. Last was an envelope with a fake I.D. in it that identified me as Sherri Bell. The I.D. had a union sticker at the lower right-hand corner. I hoped that would keep union police from killing me on sight.

I came out and was startled to see another man with the coyote. The man didn't even glance at me. He tore the security uniform out of my hands and stuffed it down a disposal chute. The coyote was already on the way out. "Go with him now," was all the coyote said.

The new guy wouldn't even talk to me. He just walked out and I followed him. He got into a hydrolift, barely giving me a chance to climb into the opposite side before he started it up and drove toward one of the open loading doors of the *Aguirré*.

If I hadn't just spent my life savings, I might have punched him right in that little self-satisfied smile he was wearing.

We drove right into the monster guts of the *Aguirré*, into a cargo deck that was as big as a warehouse. Once we had stopped, the guy looked around to make sure we were alone, and crooked his finger at me. I got down from the hydrolift and followed him to some storage lockers. He pulled one open. It looked full.

"Stay in there until I let you out," he said.

"You've got to be kidding. There's no room in there."

"Sure there is," he said, and he pushed me in. Most of my body didn't want to fit. He shoved the padded door against my backside. Had to throw all his weight against it. I would have laughed if I hadn't been so mad and scared. It was just impossible.

But with a final shove that made my ribs feel like they were cracking, he got the door latched. My butt must have sunk four inches into the door padding.

"You'll be safer in there," he called through the door. "Anywhere else, the G-forces might kill you!"

I heard him laugh as he walked away.

In my head, a little story was spinning itself. The Captain and crew of the *Aguirré* are sad to report that they discovered the body of a stowaway in one of the cargo lockers. The stowaway evidently had not known that the G-forces of takeoff would kill her unless she was strapped into a horizontal, specially padded chair. Every bone in her body was broken, and indeed it was difficult even to tell what sex she had been—

I could see the coyote and the pig who had locked me in there laughing over my money as they counted it, and talking about how gullible these runaways are. *Too bad they never get to tell tales.*

But I couldn't move at all. I think I must have waited a couple of hours before I felt the ship moving out onto the field. And for the first time it occurred to me to wonder if they kept this part of the ship pressurized when they thought no one was in there.

Then I felt the G-forces of takeoff, and all I thought about was pain.

My knees began to buckle immediately. Thank God the stuff in there with me gave before my bones did. Pretty soon I was kneeling on the debris of boxes, cartons, food rations, and a large quantity of styrofoam packing, with my head on my knees. And then the G-forces let up.

I could still breathe. I didn't know if it was because there was still air left in the locker—but not the cargo deck—or if the air pressure was on all over the ship. The artificial gravity felt weird. Once the relief wore off, I was angry again. But after a few more hours of waiting I was just tired.

Finally the door flew open, and a big man with a face right out of a twentieth century Western vid grinned in at me.

"Well! What's this?" he said.

I wasn't sure I wanted to come out anymore. He may have had a hero's face, but a rat was looking out through his eyes.

"I'm Bell," I said. "I'm new."

I came out of the locker after all.

"I can see that." The way he looked at me made my skin crawl. I was still chubby and pimply then, but I was also at his mercy, and maybe that's what turned him on.

"I'm Conners," he said. "You can call me Captain. Your gear is over *there*. You're already late for your shift."

Bastard hadn't bothered to get me out in time for supper. But I made up for it at breakfast. I learned the ropes fast, especially those that pertained to food and heavy work. And after a few months of being stared at by overaged underachievers who thought it might be fun to fuck a Runaway, I bought myself a pair of shades from the ship's general store. Once my best features were under cover, they lost interest.

Except for Captain Conners. He turned out to be a real problem.

I finally got to sleep in Blackie's "guest room" just after dawn. The light comforted me like it used to when I was a little kid who thought there was a monster under the bed. I didn't even dream about the Lyrri-dog, and when Farouk woke me early, I didn't mind. I had been dreaming about the *Aguirré,* which was almost as bad, and I was happy to be interrupted.

"Let's get out of here while she's still asleep," he said. I agreed.

Blackie's place isn't far from the fast-food stalls. Or the Spacer Sector either—she's about an equal distance from both, maybe a forty-five minute walk. She likes to be at the center of things.

The food stalls were packed with the breakfast crowd. Prospects looked good.

"Here's the first rule," I told Farouk. "What gets left on the tables is yours. What gets tossed in the trash belongs to the Skids, and they'll try to kill you if you go near it."

He nodded, looking at the sea of concrete tables. Tinkers were already glaring at us, so I nudged him and moved on.

Some government workers got up, leaving their leftovers for scavengers. Before I could say a word, Farouk had darted over and scored, getting the drop on some more experienced Deadtowners. One came after him.

"Hey, kid—!"

Farouk gave him a fairly good approximation of The Look and stuffed the food into his mouth. For a little guy, he's got nerve. He just might make it.

"Hey Shade," someone called. "You hangin' out with Babies again?"

I ignored it. Farouk didn't seem to catch it. We moved to another stall. More tinkers and government workers. And of course, Deadtowners and Skids. Farouk and I split up and made our way around opposite ends.

Bingo! Half a sub in sight.

Another government worker was abandoning her food. I was the closest to it, so I went like an arrow.

A tinker at a nearby table caught sight of me and what I was doing. He casually reached over and picked up the sandwich. Then, looking me straight in the eye, he tossed it into a gutter full of green, slimy water. His friends laughed.

I was scoping like I always do in crowds. And I was looking in this bastard's eyes, and for a moment I caught a glimpse of the way he saw me and other Deadtowners. I saw myself as something sub-human, inferior, something to be crushed under his bootheel. My eyes fogged over with red.

He turned his back on me and stuffed more of his breakfast into his face.

My body felt like a lectrowhip.

"HEY, MOTHERFUCKER!" I screamed with a voice two octaves higher than usual. He didn't turn around, but his friends were watching me. I grabbed a drink from a government worker and threw it at the back of his head. Right on target.

He jumped up and faced me, white and big-eyed with rage. I already had my knives out. I scoped. He was a bully with too much fat around his waist. Weak on the left side. Overconfident. I was going to carve him up good.

He lunged at me and I got in several slashes to his face and hands. I could have done his throat, but I wanted satisfaction. All those days of living hard and not knowing who my friends were— and this pig thought he was better than me.

I ducked under some very good right crosses and jabbed at his stomach and side, scoring every time with both knives. I was going strong. I was going to win.

And that's when the other two tinkers jumped me.

I was hit in the head and stomach a few times, but not too much, because Farouk and some other Deadtowners jumped in to save my ass. And that's how the riot started.

This was pretty much how it was divided: tinkers and a few government workers on one side (though most of those G-workers wisely ran away), and Deadtowners and Skids on the other.

Maybe the Skids joined in because a sandwich in the gutter can't be eaten by *anyone*, or maybe because so many of them are Ragnir vets and they miss the action. Either way, I know they're sick of being spit on by tinkers. They inflicted some pretty heavy mayhem.

The tinker who tossed the sandwich was stomped into the ground before I could get back to him, so I just cut any other tinker who got in my way. It was murder. Lots of people were going down, but I didn't care. Finally someone yelled, "Watch it! The dogs!" That woke me up.

Farouk was already pulling at my arm. I followed him. We ran past a clump of Skids and around a corner—right smack into a familiar face.

Chaz.

His eyes locked onto mine like a death ray, and I backpedalled out of his reach. Time stretched almost to the breaking point as I tried to make my feet work again. I thought he whispered, "Shade . . ."

"Come on!" Farouk yanked me into a stumble. "They're coming!" Chaz's eyes flicked to him for a second, and I was released.

The two of us raced away, Farouk from the dogs and me from something a lot worse. I think Farouk was curious as to why I continued to run even after the noise had died down. When I was finally convinced that Chaz wasn't following us, we turned toward Blackie's place and walked the rest of the way.

"Thanks for the lesson," Farouk said.

I laughed, but he looked serious.

"You're somethin' else," he said. "I want to be like you."

"Don't talk like that," I said. The elation was beginning to wear off. Strange feelings were creeping in. I was wondering what Knossos would think of what I had done.

Blackie and Jake were still asleep, so Farouk and I raided the kitchen. I was glad when he didn't say anything more about how great I was.

I'm back on the eighth floor, trying to ignore the noise from downstairs and the nonsense from everyone about how mean and dangerous we all are because we slaughtered the tinkers. Blackie was all over me, and now Jake hates me more than ever. No one seems to remember how the

Skids helped us out. Or they don't want to remember.

Deadtowners think I'm crazy for eating with the Skids. Deadtowners and Skids can barely stand each other. But I like the old-timers, and not just because of Knossos. Eating with them is like having dinner with your grandparents. They ask you why you cut your hair so funny and talk about the old days. Since many of them are veterans, they have something to talk about. I learned what I know about the Ragnir War from them.

"In school they told us the Ragnir War was a *conflict*," I told Knossos one night. That got me some interesting looks around the table at the Salvation Army. Even Snag was quiet.

Knossos said, "It was a war."

"You humans call it conflict because you lose face," Snag put in. "You supposed to be peace-mongers, not financing one side in foreign war."

I watched Knossos. He was staring over our heads with more hate than I'd known he could feel. I almost wanted to turn around to see who he was looking at, but I knew it wasn't someone in the room with us. The people in Hollywood might think the war ended ten years ago, but Knossos was still on the battlefield.

"How brave and noble their words were at the start," he said, "until we no longer suited their purposes."

"You should have gotten it in writing," I said.

When he glared at me I had to look away from the pain in his eyes. "If an oath has no meaning," he said, "scribbles on paper have even less."

I was ashamed of myself then, and I don't like to feel that way, so I pretended to be busy with my supper.

"Shade," he said. "I have a little money. I am in a betting mood."

I almost nodded my head off. We'd been to the pits together only once, and won bigger than I'd ever dreamed possible. I'd only used my talent alone before that, and with Knossos along I seemed to be able to focus it better. I'd been trying to get him to take me back for months.

Snag chattered at us for the rest of the meal about who was popular and who we should bet on. I ignored him.

Knossos and I rode down to the Q'rin fields, and no one gave us any trouble. It was amazing how differently people treated me when I was with him. I was so excited I could hardly keep my face on straight, and after we were seated I gave up trying. Knossos and I had to sit at the back of the Q'rin section because they're the only ones who have seats big enough for him to sit in. Fortunately they have the best view of the pit.

The Q'rin nearby pointedly ignored us, but other people stared. Some of them were laughing. It burned me to imagine what they were thinking. In all the time I have lived in Capital, I have never been propositioned by an alien whose race I did not closely resemble. I've never even thought of sleeping with Knossos. I don't think it's physically possible. The idea was embarrassing.

"Shade," Knossos said, "let others think what they will."

I must have turned bright red, because he laughed. It was the first time I ever heard a sound like that from him. "I would like to think that we are partners," he said.

"I'm glad," I said. "I want that too."

Everyone got quiet when the announcer walked to the center of the astroturf. He was an old Q'rin whose face was a mask of battle scars. He turned a full circle, regarding the crowd with his one good eye. "First fight," he said. "Krell and Timmy, lectrowhips." There was a cheer from the Lyrri side of the audience as the fighters came out from opposite doors in the pit walls. Lyrri love the elegant kills.

"Place your bets," said the announcer. "You have ten units."

I scoped Timmy and Krell. Timmy was a Lyrri, and she kept pulling my eyes back. But Krell looked like he was hiding some danger.

I got as clear a picture as I could on my own, then turned to my partner. "Timmy is current champion," he said. "She is faster, and has a powerful overcut. But she is weaker with left-handed opponents, and Krell is left-handed. He is new but very talented."

I watched him while he watched them, and made my decision.

"Timmy," I said.

Knossos hailed the recorder. He entered our names and our bet into the central computer and collected our money. I squirmed in my seat and wished for a bag of peanuts.

"Time," the announcer said. He walked through his own door, leaving Timmy and Krell alone in the pit.

They switched their whips on and swished them back and forth overhead like electronic cobras as the charge built up higher and higher, making them harder to control as each moment passed. They had to keep moving, or the whips would have been drawn right back to them, wrapping themselves around their users and emptying their charge, burning right through to the bone. I saw an amateur die that way once. They would have to use the damn things soon, or the whips would become uncontrollable; but they just circled each other lazily, their lectrowhips humming.

Krell's whip licked out and touched the left side of Timmy's face in a wicked undercut. She grinned with the side of her mouth that wasn't burned, and things suddenly got fast and furious.

I had almost forgotten what a lectrowhip fight between two masters looked like, because I hardly ever see the whip used on the streets. I won't ever forget that fight, though. Timmy still hadn't used her charge, and her whip was moving back and forth in the air like electrons around a nucleus, burning strange afterimages in my vision. Krell was dancing back and forth, watching for her move and waiting for his own charge to build back up. He must have been horribly tense, but he didn't show it. I felt like I was watching a ballet; and it was so beautiful, I forgot how deadly it must be.

Timmy reminded me as she struck like a cobra and caught Krell around the neck. Her whip was so charged up that it lifted him off his feet. His whip dropped to the ground and writhed there, as he danced at the end of hers like some horrible puppet.

She let him hang until most of her charge was gone, then flipped him backward onto the fire rods that line the sides of the pit. The rods are there to discourage people from running up the incline. They burned his body to a crisp in seconds. He must have been dead by that time anyway. I was glad I hadn't eaten any peanuts. I don't think the Q'rin who sat in front of me would have enjoyed cleaning them off his head.

Timmy switched her whip off and strolled from the pit, oblivious to the cheers of the crowd, dragging the whip in the dust behind her. No one bothered to fetch Krell's body. They wouldn't do that until the fights were over for the day. The smell of his cooked flesh filled my nostrils as I calculated our winnings.

We had doubled our credits. If we could continue to win, we would make a tidy sum. I scoped the next two contestants, and this time it was easier. They were Deadtown knife fighters.

I don't know when the Q'rin sitting next to me started to catch on. Maybe he was the one who tipped off Donokh. By the third fight he was betting on the same people. Knossos ignored him, and I took his lead. As far as I know there's no rule against my particular talent. I was more worried about Knossos. His brown eyes had turned red.

The last fight was announced. We'd won the previous seven, and I thought we ought to withdraw. The last fight is usually wrestling; and because it's not as deadly, some of the crowd usually leaves. But Knossos sat like a rock. And for some reason, everyone else did the same.

"Ousa and Rorra," the announcer called, "wrestling. Last fight of the evening, fifteen units to place your bets."

Fifteen units seemed a bit excessive. Until I scoped the fighters and became confused for the first time that evening.

Ousa and Rorra were Aesopians. All of the pit wrestlers are, because no one else could possibly go up against an Aesopian in any kind of hand-to-hand combat and win. Ousa was a lion man, and Rorra was a bear man. They were approximately the same height, weight, and had the same reach. They looked to be in perfect condition, like warriors. Their fur was glossy, and the sharp teeth that peeked out from their drawn lips looked white and strong. They reminded me of someone.

I looked sideways at the elephant man. He knew them. Not just casually, either. Somehow, they were kin. And the expression in his eyes told me that this was not the time to ask about it.

"Ousa is stronger," he was saying, "but Rorra is slippery and more tenacious."

"Rorra," I said.

We bet the whole bundle. And we won.

The morning after the riot I avoided the fast-food stalls. So did every other Deadtowner. Rumors had trickled in that those ex-tinker human-dogs were just itching to make us Deadtowners wish we really were dead. You would think my pals would be furious with me for making life harder than usual. But instead they think I'm some kind of hero for defending Deadtown honor against the hated tinkers.

Last night Blackie had a big party to celebrate. You could tell it was a party instead of just the usual crowd, because Blackie kept announcing it every five minutes.

"And Shade is the queen of the party," she said when she noticed I was about to sneak away, "because she's the ultimate Deadtowner!!"

Everyone looked at me with as much approval as Deadtowners ever muster for anyone, and drank, smoked, or stimmed themselves to my health.

I guess they don't know *ultimate* means *last.*

"Here." Farouk passed me another stick of killer loki and tried to look nonchalant, but I could see the worship in his eyes, even behind the shades he's taken to wearing. I bet he would even sleep with me now if I wanted him to.

I'm not so happy about what happened. If it had just been me and that lousy tinker, I would have felt better. I was so focused on him I didn't scope how everyone else was getting heated up. Dumb.

So I waited until Blackie passed out, which was fortunately earlier than usual, and got myself a good night's sleep. I went to the S.A. for breakfast the next morning. Cut through the Spacer Sector, past the casinos, and back into Midtown and Skid territory. There were a lot more Skids in line than usual. Guess they're keeping away from the dogs too. They held their own pretty well at the riot. I wondered if Mira and Snag had been there, had seen what I did. I sort of hoped not.

Knossos always sits with Mira at the S.A., and sometimes they talk as if they've known each other for years. He always treats her with respect. I didn't see either one of them in line, but I hoped they might be inside.

Well, Mira was, anyway. Snag too. I sat with them and ate my gruel and biscuits. I was almost finished before I noticed that Snag wasn't shooting his mouth off as usual. He was looking at me out of the corner of one eye.

"What's going on?" I asked.

"Finish your breakfast," he said. He wouldn't

say anything else. Mira seemed to ignore us both. I choked down the rest of the gruel. "Okay," I said. "What is it?"

Mira looked me right in the eye.

"I thought you should know," she said. "Last night some Q'rin-dogs raided the Baby School. Most everyone there was asleep, so they didn't make it out the bolt-holes. They were all killed."

I didn't feel anything for several seconds. "Huh?" I said. "Why?"

"I hear one of the Lords ordered it," she said. "Something about how the Baby School was being used by human-dogs to store weapons. Some are saying it was a threat so close to Q'rin territory. Two of the other Lords countermanded the order, but by then it was too late—"

I can't remember anything else she said, or what I said back. All I can remember is that relentless truth in her worn face, and how she wouldn't look away when I started to cry.

Dead Baby faces talk to me as I'm trying to write this, and blow loki smoke like the pros they really were. I can't see them with their eyes glazed over and turned up in their heads. Can't see Stone that way, or Lilo, or Ramona.

I don't know if there were weapons stored there or not. But if there were, why did they have to kill the children? Why couldn't they have waited for the place to fill up with Johns and killed them instead?

I'm back on the eighth floor. I sat with Mira and Snag until all the tears ran out and my face dried up. Then I came here, taking a lot more trouble than usual to stay in the shadows. I kept seeing Q'rin-dogs out of the corner of my eye, force guns in their big, hard hands. Or Lyrri-dogs with sweet smiles who wanted to talk *business*.

I had been sitting here for hours trying to get my brain back to some kind of normal function when the obvious finally occurred to me. I guess living on Z'taruh for a couple of years has turned me into a ghoul. But it makes sense. It's horrible, but the death of the Babies presents me with a peculiar opportunity. It doesn't even matter that I made such a spectacle of myself at the riot, or that I ran right into Chaz afterward. Because as far as he knows, *I died in that raid with the Babies.* I intend to start a rumor to that effect immediately.

Hey, it's a chance.

I wonder if Lilo was sleeping next to Stone when he died. I don't want to think about what they must have done to that little guy.

As for Stone, I'm glad he didn't die in some snuff-vid.

More noise from downstairs. Everyone acting like they own the planet. No one gives a shit that the Babies are dead. But I'm glad for the noise. Tonight I don't want to be alone.

Last night I dreamed I was back on the *Aguirré*. Captain Conners was hassling me. He wanted more than just to fuck me; he was acting out some strange story in his own head where he was the hero and I was some difficult task he had to perform. But his hero's hat kept slipping off.

I was eight months into the job and I still hadn't left the ship. That's rather like being in a maximum security prison for eight months, just dying to get your feet on growing grass and breathe free air. Only Conners could issue the I.D.s that were good for off-ship use, and he wouldn't. Always, just before we were about to go into orbit, he would make it a point to work alone with me, doing something close, like in the duct system or something. In my dream there seemed to be no end to the duct system, no way to get away from him. He was breathing in my face, and I could smell the old fillings in his teeth.

"You want to go planet-side?" he asked me.

I didn't want to answer, because I remembered what he was likely to say to me. But thinking something and saying something in a dream can be the same thing.

"Yes!"

"I tell you what, then," he said. "Come on back with me to my quarters, and you can sit on my face and suck my cock."

He looked so aroused when he said it, like he was sure it would arouse me too. I laughed in his face.

I thought I woke up. I was lying in some trash. I had no I.D. and no money. The *Aguirré* logo had been stripped off the front of my coveralls. I was an illegal immigrant to Z'taruh, and I was truly scared.

Suddenly Knossos was there, staring down at me in my pile of trash. "Why are you afraid?" he asked. "You are here because you want to be."

That thought woke me up for real. I had to sit up and think about it some more. I'm here. Not Shade and Sherri Bell or any other name I call myself or get called. *I'm* here. It's not enough just to spread a rumor that Shade was killed in the Baby School raid, because Chaz and Donokh will still be looking at *me*. I have to change my looks.

Think I'll just turn into someone else for a while.

Blackie couldn't wait to dress me up. I haven't seen her so happy since the old days. She always wanted to dress me up back then, but I resisted. It had just seemed too convenient to me, and I couldn't understand why she was offering me this free ride. Later I realized that it wasn't free at all, and the dress-up thing was part of the control I was relinquishing.

Now I was asking for it. Her eyes got all shiny when I told her what I wanted.

"Really?" she asked in a little girl voice. "Don't lie to me."

"Why the hell should I lie?" She flinched, so I changed my tactics. "Blackie, when have I ever lied?"

"Never. You were the only one who never lied."

"I'm asking you because you know exactly what I want. You're an expert."

She didn't exactly like the compliment. Maybe she thought I was making fun of her and didn't really mean it. But she grabbed my arm and pulled me into her big dressing room. It looked like an overstuffed costume shop. I felt a sharp pang of envy, despite myself.

"Where's Jake?" I asked casually.

"He's out showing Farouk how to pick pockets."

Like hell. Jake is the most selfish, uncharitable soul on this entire planet. And he's jealous of Farouk. The kid was out teaching himself, like he's supposed to.

"I want to look like a G-worker's kid," I said. "You know, self-conscious fashion, ruffles, lots of glow jewelry."

She already had an armload of stuff for me to try on. I was in her hands. It was going to be a long session.

A lot of the stuff she tried on me looked brand new. She must have reconciled with her family again. Rich bitch to the core. Can't stand Mom and Dad, but the money just keeps flowing, and somehow that's all right. I swear I'd like to meet her folks some day. Would be interesting to scope the power that feeds the human-dogs.

I made my body go limp as she turned me into a mannequin. If I had resisted even slightly, moved right when she wanted me left, I would have gotten bruised for my trouble. She was in heaven playing with her very own live doll, the madonna smile on her lips.

"I wish I were skinny like you," she said as she pinned a skirt to take up the slack.

"You're fine the way you are," I said.

She is. She's ten times more beautiful than I could ever hope to be. Creamy olive skin, midnight-black eyes. She doesn't need sculpted eyes.

"I'm going to need to borrow some of your shades to disguise my eyes," I said.

She pouted and stopped what she was doing for a moment. "Why are you such a shithead?"

"Huh?"

"I thought you were going to let me fix you over."

"Yeah."

When I didn't say anything more, she shook her head. Same old argument, same old result. She stuffed a wig over my head and started to mess with it.

"I really missed you—you know?" she said. "I

mean—can I be honest with you? I mean—really honest?"

"Yes."

She made a sound that was halfway between a cough and a laugh. She was really tense. "I mean—okay. Honesty time here. Real heavy shit. I just—you know—thought you really hated me."

"You were wrong" (Sometimes I can be a real bitch.)

"It's just—" she tugged at the wig, almost pulling it off my head—"the last time I talked to you. We—like—almost cut each other's heads off. And—I just thought you hated me."

"We were mad at each other. We had a fight. Do you hate me for that?" I asked.

"It's like—sometimes I just can feel the hate rays coming off you. And I wanna say, 'come on Shade—I'm treading water as fast as I can!'"

"Hate rays?"

And it's like—you always said that one day I would—flake out for the last time. And that would be it. Just—it."

"So, now I'm back."

"Yeah, you are. And I just—like—want to know where I stand."

She tore the wig off as if she really weren't concerned about the answer and replaced it with another one. She acted like she hadn't even brought up the subject in the first place.

"You stand where you've always stood," I said. "Where you damn well please."

Silence for a moment, and busy hands. Then, "Really?"

"Yes."

"Because there's just one thing I can't stand.

And that's for someone I love to turn around and hate me."

I mumbled something, hoping that would be the end of it. But then she whipped out the black nail polish.

Here's where I got to prove that I really didn't hate her. If I wanted to live with Blackie, I'd have to wear Blackie's mark. I sighed and extended my hands.

And there was one other thing.

"Come with me to the casinos tonight," she said.

"I can't tonight. We'll go tomorrow night."

She gave me the madonna smile, the I've-got-you-under-my-thumb curling of the lips that always made me nervous. For a moment the Blackie static faded and I got a glimpse of her insides, saw the feverish delight she felt over the situation. I was almost glad when the static came back.

When I found Mira at the Salvation Army she didn't recognize me at first. She looked right through me until she realized I wasn't going to go away. Then she gave me a stony grimace that would have done a Q'rin proud.

"Where's Knossos?" I asked her. I had decided to lay it on the line.

"Around somewhere," she said.

"Well, where's Snag?"

"At the bottom of Smoke River."

"Shit." I sat down and tried to think what to do next. I had walked over to the S.A. feeling like a new woman, confident and safe from my enemies in my new disguise. I was ready to go get some action at the pits; and even though I hadn't expected to find Knossos, I had at least thought Snag would be around. I needed a partner. Now what? I looked at Mira and she looked back. Suddenly she smiled with one corner of her mouth.

"Very few people would recognize you dressed that way," she said. "You have a scheme?"

"A money scheme," I said. "I wanna go bet at the pits. You ever do that?"

"I do. I used to be a pit fighter myself."

"No kidding!"

I almost turned into a goofy fan right on the spot. I always knew there was something about Mira. She didn't have any scars, but I believed her.

"You busy today?" I asked her.

So in no time the two of us were on a tran and on our way to the pits. We passed the time talking about our favorite fighters.

"I like Larissa," she told me. "She's fast and graceful. I used to fight in the knife categories myself, though I did some mangler fighting too."

I figured her body under those rags must be a real sight. I was proud she was even talking to me.

Lots of promising pockets were on that transport, but I resisted them. Soon Mira and I were out the door and walking across the field to the pits. The animal show was still going strong, and the place was still extra crowded. So far so good. We strolled up to the gate, and damned if we didn't run into Donokh.

He and some other Q'rin-dog planted themselves right in front of us. I was so startled I just froze. Mira locked a hand around my wrist before I could turn and run.

They just stood there. Donokh was frowning, but I didn't see any recognition in his eyes.

"No humans allowed," he snapped.

"Bullshit," said Mira.

"We're cracking down," Donokh said. "We don't want your kind around."

"Too bad," said Mira, "because we're staying."

I was beginning to catch on. This was typical Q'rin behavior. They were just getting their jollies from intimidating us. I hadn't gone through this at the pits before because Knossos had always been with me.

I could tell they liked Mira's style. I kept my mouth shut, but Donokh glanced at me again, and this time I saw a flicker of suspicion in his eyes.

"I've seen you before," he said. His hand started toward my shades.

Suddenly Mira was screaming at him in Q'rin. He and the other guy almost jumped out of their skins. Their heavy-jawed mouths hung open with astonishment. She spat several phrases at them until Donokh finally held his hands up placatingly. He shot me one last glance and the two of them turned their backs on us. A challenge. We didn't take it, but we didn't have to. Face was saved all around.

Mira pulled me through the gate. "Do you know him?" she asked me.

"Yeah. You think he recognized me?"

"I don't know. Q'rin men have an accute sense of smell. He might have recognized you that way."

Well, the hell with him. Tomorrow I'll be someone else. And I'll be at the stupid casinos, where Q'rin men hardly ever go.

"You sure speak their language well," I said.

"That's easy." She pulled some credits out of a pocket at her waist and paid the ticket man. "Now Earth Standard—*that's* a tough language."

I paid the man for my own ticket and scurried after her. She went straight for the oddball section, snagging us a couple of seats as close to pitside as she could get.

The place filled up rapidly. I felt great.

"I hear you have a special talent for betting on the right fighters," said Mira. "I'd like to see for myself."

"That's what I'm here for," I said.

We waited for the scarred announcer to silence the place with his entrance. He came out and looked the crowd over.

"First fight," he said. "Karen and Larissa, double knife."

Two Deadtown girls came out and faced each other. Larissa must have been six feet tall. Her black skin was a perfect blend with her ragwraps. She had long, powerful arms. Karen had orange hair and an overbite. She was about five-foot-four. They drew two knives each out of upper arm sheaths and waited.

"Place your bets," said the announcer. "You have fifteen units."

Larissa scoped pretty tough. She had a better reach and looked fast. I turned to Mira.

"As I told you before, Larissa is my favorite. But she doesn't believe she can lose, and lately she has been overconfident. The little orange-haired one is as vicious as a three-tailed scorpion."

Yow! I got such a clear picture of what she saw, I knew exactly who to choose. "Karen," I said. "This time, anyway."

Larissa really was overconfident. She had this

attitude like "Lets get this over with before you bore me to death." She had the moves to back up that arrogance, and glided around Karen like a dancer. But Karen was a seething mass of hate inside, and I could feel her about to explode a few seconds before she actually did. They had been feinting at each other, sort of checking each other out before that moment, when Karen suddenly lunged in and sliced Larissa's ear off.

You should have seen the look on Larissa's face. She was proud of her looks and prouder of her fighting ability. She lost her temper, and the two of them just started slicing at each other. It reminded me of the fight Katie and I had over the Chocolate Doodle Cake, only ten times meaner. They hit each other's arms, torsos, and hands so many times I could barely keep count. Larissa expended some energy trying to protect her face, but other than that, they just didn't care.

Finally the ref stepped in and shouted, "Hold!"

They ignored him. So he and three other big Q'rin threw stun nets over Larissa and Karen. The two women were dragged from the ring. The ref looked up at the judges and got a signal from them.

"Karen is the winner," he said. Some people cheered, but most seemed disappointed. Especially the men. Larissa really is good looking.

Anyway, once she cools off, I bet she considers that fight a good lesson. She won't be easy to beat again, that's for sure.

The next fight was almost ready to start. I was scoping through Mira at the fighters, two Q'rin lectrowhippers, when I started to see a weird double image. I could have sworn there was a Q'rin woman sitting next to me. Then it was

Mira again, but I was seeing her differently. She studied those two men like the pro she was.

"Abraa is stronger," she said. "Kortris is faster."

And Mira was a Q'rin. I was sure of it.

We ended up in a Skid bar after the fights, one of those places where you can buy homemade booze and meltdown real cheap. Now that I thought I knew something about Mira, everything she said seemed to have at least two meanings. She could drink almost as much as Knossos, so she got a little friendlier than usual.

"Lord Knossos was right about you," she told me.

Lord Knossos! "Really?" I said.

"You're good. You know what to look for. I like the money you earned for me tonight." She patted the pouch at her waist and smiled.

"Likewise," I said. I didn't have to fake the smile back. "We'll have to do it again sometime."

She nodded, but her eyes were already focusing on something else. Her face got rock hard. I scoped in the direction she was looking and saw another Skid. He was a rangy, big-mouthed human.

"Those mother-rapers are animals," he was saying. "Fucking vermin. I fought ten years in that mother-raping war, and now I got to look at their ugly faces every day. What was it all for, man?"

It was another bigot sounding off about the Aesopians. I hear that all the time. Lots of human soldiers look down on the Aesopians. Can't figure out why they had to fight for and along with them.

"I mean the way they strut around town. Makes

me wish I was back on Ragnir with a force rifle. Burn their big ugly heads off. I mean it. Right between those hairy eyebrows."

Mira was really hating this guy. But she was completely composed. Wish I had that kind of control.

"You and Knossos are old friends, huh?" I asked her.

"Old comrades," she snapped.

"Even their broads are ugly," Bigmouth was saying. "That's why they attacked us. They wanted some good-looking pussy for a change." He laughed and so did his friends.

I had been wrong. He was talking about the Q'rin. I suddenly pictured Donokh with his hand on my knee. The back of my neck got real hot.

I thought Mira would be even madder, but she just laughed when he said Q'rin women were ugly.

"I'd give anything to be *ugly* like that again," she said. "Let me tell you something little girl. I had knife scars on both cheeks and up and down my arms. I had lectrowhip burns. And I was proud. But then I traded it for *this*." She tugged at her face like it was a mask. "This smooth, half-baked face. These weak hands. I was a good soldier once."

"You had plastic surgery?" I asked.

She shook her head. "I'll tell you what it was. I know you'll keep it to yourself, just as you know I won't speak to that Lyrri-dog who keeps asking about you." She looked me in the eye, and suddenly I wished I hadn't asked.

"You know I'm Q'rin," she said. "I can see that. I joined the navy when the war started, gave up my promising career as a fighter. I was young and patriotic. Never thought I would end up as a spy.

"I infiltrated Lord Knossos's ship. For him I turned traitor." She stabbed a finger at the loudmouth. "Or for *that* animal, depending on how you look at it."

"Uh, well—the Q'rin won the war anyway," I said.

"By default. Not by clean victory. It left a bad taste in the mouth. It was shameful."

Privately that's always been my opinion, too.

"I know what it's like to be in disguise," she said, "but my flesh is my disguise." She leaned forward and grabbed my collar, pulling me close.

"RNA virus," she said.

I must have shown her a blank face.

"This body is human," she said. "Its memories destroyed and its brain imprinted with mine. My own brain was destroyed in the process, along with my body of course."

She released me and leaned back, taking a couple of long pulls on her drink. I was busy trying to absorb what she had just told me.

"I've never been able to quite grasp the fact that I'm dead," she said.

It was the last thing she said all night.

I couldn't get Mira to leave with me. She didn't even respond to my voice. I didn't push it.

I took a roundabout way back to Blackie's place. I looked too much like a government brat to take chances. On the way home I passed the Baby School. It was all boarded up. I swear I could smell the death in there. I still can't believe they're all gone.

Farouk looked at me funny when I came in. But he still shared his loki with me. He's even learned to wrap his legs up properly. Right now I can see his feet through the doorway of his room. The kid has big feet.

I'm glad I have this notebook. I can get all this junk out of my head and get some sleep. In the morning after Farouk leaves, I always have a couple hours to myself. I write and think about what's going on.

Anyway, now I know more about Knossos. Think I'll keep an eye on Mira and Snag from now on.

RNA virus. That's kind of what this notebook is. It's a weird thought.

Most humans don't understand a thing about the Aesopians. We ought to be the first to remember Aesop was a human legend—the philospher who told stories about animals who acted like people—but we aren't. Never occurs to us that the whole universe isn't designed after the human pattern.

And that's probably why we never wonder how come the Aesopians look like they're descended from Earth animals. Once I heard some tinkers talking about it. "Yeah," this one guy says, "it's evolution. Only instead of being descended from cavemen, they're descended from animals. Lions and bears and stuff."

Only there are no lions or bears on any of the planets we've explored so far. At least, that's what I learned in school and from the vid. There are animals that are *sort of* like big cats or bears, or a combination of both, and so on. But nothing we've found so far resembles Earth bears, lions, African elephants, cobras, wolves, etc., nearly as much as the Aesopians do.

Pretty damn strange.

Like how come when we started calling them Aesopians they adopted the name for themselves? I don't even know what they used to be called. And they won't say.

After I knew Knossos for a while I asked him, "How come you look like an elephant?"

"Because I am an elephant man," he answered.

"I know that. Why are you avoiding the question?"

"It was such a imprecise question. It wasn't what you meant to ask, I can tell. But what else can I possibly say?"

"Look," I said. "I read about your DNA experiments. I know you people used to look different before you changed yourselves to look like you do now—"

"Our ancestors changed themselves."

"Right. But how come you look so—*Earth*-like? Did you have elephants on your planet?"

"That doesn't matter now. *My* ancestors were patterned after the god Korbor. He is the god of wisdom and war."

"Strange combination."

"For your people, not for mine."

"But how come you won't tell me if there were elephants on your planet?"

"The Great War destroyed so much of our works and our habitat, long before my line was established. Most of our history before that time is legend."

"Is that a yes or a no?"

"Neither."

We had a lot of talks like that. I don't think he was trying to avoid my questions. I really believe he answered as well as he could. In fact, he told me a lot about his people, more than I ever could have learned in school. I know who his ancestors are, all the way back to The Change. I know the names of the gods they changed themselves to resemble. That sort of thing. But he wouldn't tell me what the Aesopians looked like before they became animal-men. Or whether or not the animals of their planet resembled Earth animals as much as it appears. Or why they call themselves Aesopians now.

I suspect it's just too personal for them to discuss. And it's probably just as well. Lord knows there are enough humans who think the Aesopians are trained animals. They wouldn't understand why the animal-men aren't insulted by the comparison. To the animal-men, humans are a mostly cowardly, dishonorable race who can make fancy weapons, but who are incabable of understanding the simplest rules of behavior.

Aesopians will show you respect until you prove you don't deserve it. It's as simple as that. You don't have to like the way they look. Just don't be an asshole.

Personally, I think the Aesopians must have had interstellar travel before The Change. They probably visited Earth and maybe even brought back some animals. Why they would worship *those* animals, I don't know. They don't think like we do.

But come to think of it, a lot of our gods don't look like anything on Earth, either. So what the hell do I know?

Farouk went out with a haunted look on his face this morning. Reminded me of my own face a couple of years ago. Back when I was starving and I was learning how many men are willing to pay for Baby ass. Even Big Baby ass.

I had my sixteenth birthday on the *Aguirré*. But I looked like a tall fourteen-year-old. No boobs. Chubby baby face. Must have driven Captain Conners crazy.

But maybe he had a good reason for refusing to let me off the ship whenever we were planetside. The Union Police probably would have spotted me for what I was, and then Conners would have been chewing icicles on Odin for ten to fifteen.

He kept hinting that a little pussy could change his mind, but I knew he wasn't that stupid. That's why I was so suspicious when he told me he was going to let me go ashore on Z'taruh.

"I hear you play poker," he said.

"A little. It's boring."

"I hear you always win."

I shrugged. It surprised me too, but I could usually tell what the other players were going to do. I tried not to win so much so the others wouldn't want to kill me.

"How'd you like to see the casinos on Z'taruh?"

That's all everyone had been talking about for the last two months. I'd never heard of the place, myself. It sounded dirty and sleazy. I really wanted to go.

"You finally going to issue me land I.D.?"

"Better than that. You can come with me."

Uh oh.

"Take it or leave it," he said.

He thought I was going to win him some money. And he wasn't asking for a blow-job first.

"Okay," I said.

"We'll pass you off as my daughter," he said.

His eyes glazed over when he said that, and I learned something I didn't want to know.

"What else do you play besides poker?" he asked me.

"Nothing."

"Okay. We'll stick to cards."

He grinned and massaged my shoulder with his big hands, already getting into the role of incestuous father.

As it turned out, the cards idea wasn't so hot.

But in the meantime, I sort of enjoyed myself. We actually landed the ship this time, something we had only done twice since we had left Earth. I guess we were going to move a lot of cargo on and off. I was amazed at how hot and sticky Z'taruh was, and at the feel of Earth-like gravity again. We put down in Capital, the only city on the planet. Pretty appropriate name, huh? *Capital* —what with all the money made and lost here. Outside the city there's nothing but marshland and swamp. That's why it's so muggy. Snag loves it.

Conners was really trying to impress me. He gave me some fancy and rather sickening young-girl type clothes, and even seemed proud of the way I looked. He took me to an expensive restaurant, where I ate a very reasonable facsimile of veal and crab, with chocolate mousse for dessert. I can still taste it. He tipped the waiter fifty percent. He was sure I was going to help him win big.

Out on the streets I saw Skids and Deadtowners, Babies and adult whores. But I didn't concern myself with them. They weren't important yet.

Dogs and tinkers stared at me. I'm glad those plump, baby-faced days are over.

So in we went to a big, bright casino. I had thought we were going to see happy, laughing people with drinks in their hands, but everyone was dead serious. No smiles. Lots of anger and frustration. Conners headed straight for a black-jack console.

"Better go for poker," I said.

"Blackjack is better."

"I can't read people with blackjack."

"Don't worry about it," he said. "Just stick with me."

He wasn't going to listen. He thought I was a winner because I was just lucky.

"We're going to do great," he said.

But we didn't.

"I thought you couldn't lose," he said, no longer smiling.

"I never said that."

He came pretty close to backhanding me then.

"Let's play poker," I said.

"It's not that simple. They have tournaments for that, and we're out of season."

"So people never get up games on their own? Shit, I could win more money than you just lost in a few games on the ship!"

He stared at me with his mouth all tight, his eyes narrowed and pulling the skin all the way to his ears.

"That's not the way I do it," he said.

"I've got to read people," I said. "*People*. Not numbers."

"You're fucking useless, you know that?"

"If we can get up a game, I'll win all your money back plus more. I swear. You *do* have some money left, don't you?"

He was holding my shoulder real tight, digging

his fingers into the nerves. He had never hurt me before. Gamblers are crazy.

"How about the rat-fights?" he said.

"Don't make me sick!"

"Look," he said, practically squeezing my arm off, "we don't have time to go sniffing around for suckers."

"Are you kidding? The big hotels are full of them. We'll hang out in the bar. They'll come to us!"

Slowly the fingers relaxed, and a smile spread across that broad face. Big white teeth shined in my eyes.

"You know all about hotel bars, huh kid? Okay, we'll give it a shot."

So off we went to the Star Lodge. It was as glitzy and phoney as the casinos. He drank whiskey and I sipped a protein drink until the sharks came swimming by. It took us all of an hour to attract five of them.

They introduced themselves, but I thought of them as Fatman, Tinker, Greenteeth, and Dogs One and Two.

Conners and I had made our plans on the way over. He played the first two hands, folding one and losing another. Then I threw a temper tantrum.

"Daddy, I'm bored!"

"You wanna go play with the one-armed bandits, Baby?"

I pouted. I'd seen my old friends back in Hollywood pout hundreds of times.

"You promised I could play poker," I said.

Conners sighed. Fatman was waiting to see what we would do. He was a first-class con man. But Tinker was getting mad.

"Send the fucking brat out for some candy, will ya?"

"You said I could play!" I whined.

"Look," Conners said. "You guys don't care, do you? Money's money."

"Fine with me," said Fatman.

Tinker gritted his teeth. The two dogs sat stony-faced and Mr. Greenteeth actually smiled at me. I liked him.

So I sat down and started to play. I started slow, and then heated up. Fatman was very impressed by then, and Greenteeth had to fold. He said goodnight, and all the warmth left the room.

"Your kid has talent," Fatman said to Conners.

"Damn right!" Conners beamed. He looked genuinely proud. "I taught her everything she knows."

"I'll bet," Dog One said under his breath.

But Tinker was getting madder and madder. He thought I was cheating, but couldn't figure out how I was doing it. I lost a couple of hands to cool him down. No good.

"Daddy!" I said. "I'm losing! I'm too tired to play anymore."

"Stretch out on the couch, Baby. I'd like to get a few hands in before we go."

Damn! Why couldn't he listen to me?

"I want to go home *now*!" I whined.

"Go lie on the fucking couch!" he snapped, right out of character.

"I'd better get my money back," Tinker said.

"Don't worry. With Daddy playing, you can't lose."

"I want my money now you little slut!" Tinker grabbed my arm and all hell broke loose.

I had no idea how violent Conners could be. It was scary. I almost felt sorry for Tinker as he got his face beat in. Fatman and Dogs One and Two just watched.

Conners dumped Tinker down the stairs and came back smiling. "Let's do it," he said.

And he lost everything I had won for him.

"Hey kid," Fatman said as he was leaving, "too bad this is my last night here. You got talent. Look me up if you're ever on Hook." But he didn't tell me his name.

Dogs One and Two had left long ago, cutting their losses, like Conners hadn't had the smarts to do.

He was depressed.

"Baby," he said, "It's been a rough night. Why don't we get a room and stay here a while."

"Why don't we get two rooms?"

He gave me a real calm look.

"No," he said.

"Then I'm going back to the ship."

"No."

"I'm not sleeping with you."

"Sleep isn't what I had in mind. You owe me."

I couldn't believe it. I started to laugh. I couldn't stop, even when his face turned white and he came for me. Not even when he was punching my face.

I woke up in an alley, in a pile of trash. Then I passed out again.

I couldn't find the *Aguirré*. It was gone and my teeny clothes were torn. Once I went up to a nice-looking lady in the Spacer Sector and asked for help, and she slapped my face. Called me a whore and told me to get away from her before she called the dogs.

I would have given anything for a human embassy where I could throw myself on their mercy and tell them what had happened to me. But there's no such thing on Z'taruh. Didn't know about the Salvation Army then. So I wandered the streets and ate garbage.

That's when Lenny the Chicken Hawk found me.

He was driving around in his own mini-tran. He had three rings on each finger and snow-white hair.

"Need a place to stay?" he asked.

I knew what he wanted. His kind had been sniffing around since the first day. But I was a lot hungrier now, and I still hadn't found that elusive embassy.

"Yeah," I said, and got in the tran. How bad could it be?

Lenny took me to his place and licked me all over for two hours. Felt like two years. Then he made me a big sandwich. While I ate it, he told me what was next.

"We'll make some vids. We can make more money that way, at least at first. At least until we can build up a clientele—"

He talked a long time, and I chewed.

Finally, he had to go out. He told me to clean myself up. He locked the door from the outside; no one could get in *or* out.

I got into the shower. While I was there, I thought about how good soap and shampoo felt. And toothpaste. And giant sandwiches. But I was in there for an hour before I felt sure all of Lenny's saliva was washed off.

When I was done, I searched the apartment. I found a bunch of clothes, all different sizes, and I changed. I found a good pair of shades. I ate two more big sandwiches.

Then I smashed a window and climbed out of there. I never went back.

I've seen Lenny around a few times since then, but I don't think he recognized me. Not after the first few weeks, anyway. His expert eyes only record useful information. He was my one and only brush with prostitution.

I think I just heard Blackie yelling at someone. Time to go pay for my room and board.

It took Blackie four hours to get ready for our date, and about fifteen minutes for her to do my wig and repaint my nails with black junk. She was flying high, her natural static snapping around her and setting my teeth on edge. Before we go she pulled out this big wad of credit.

"I see you're back in good with your family," I said.

That little madonna smile came, and I could tell she felt like slapping me.

"I earned this myself," she said sweetly.

I never could figure out how Blackie gets her money. She doesn't sell her ass or her drugs; she gives them away. She doesn't work. She says her family doesn't give her anything, but she still goes to see them sometimes. And she spends what she has like there's no limit to it.

"If you want to make money instead of losing it, come with me to the pits," I told her.

"You know how I feel about violence," she said.

"No, I don't. I've seen you get into fights."

"I don't like to see people hurting each other. It's like—you know? I can just think of better things people could be doing with each other."

She put dark red on her madonna mouth and smeared her lips together.

Well, maybe she really believes that. But I've seen her inflict more emotional violence on her *friends* than I've ever seen done physically in the pits. Except for the Manglers.

"How about poker then?" I said half-heartedly. But it was no go. Blackie was looking to see and be seen. She wanted the drug-thrill of chance and didn't want a sure thing. Or she still wanted something for nothing, but wasn't willing to hand over the controls to me.

So, nails glistening blackly and hair clashing with our clothes, the two of us stepped out as rich brats. The Deadtowners know Blackie; she pays protection money so there wasn't any hassling or robbing. Me, I had my knives hidden but accessible, just in case. We hopped a transport and we were off to the only part of Z'taruh most visitors ever see.

Blackie's into roulette. She loves to lean over the table with her boots spilling out, and look at the pretty black and red squares, trying to guess which one is the magic one. Within minutes everyone is laughing and joking with her, gathering around her like long-lost buddies. This time was no exception. I didn't mind. I just stepped back and watched people, happy to be out of the static and nonsense range.

Blackie was a little luckier than usual today, losing only about half of her money. And it took her five hours to do it. While she played, I wondered why she always wants me to come along. She always forgets me after the first few moments and concentrates on making new friends. But that's the problem—she doesn't know how to keep them. After the first few hours she stops expending effort altogether, and it's up to you to keep it going.

I swear, there were three men and two women at that table who each thought she was going to make love to them later. One of them would even have been willing to marry her. But she was just there to play, and finally she got bored and hungry.

"Let's go to Medusa's," she said, grabbing my arm and hauling me along in her wake. She had cut one of her admirers off mid-sentence, and he was staring after us with a mixture of hurt feelings and resentment. Blackie saw nothing but the pretty lights and the flashing consoles. She was throwing sparks.

Me, I was choking on the idea of Medusa's. Lyrri hang out there. Some Q'rin, too. It's an overlap place between all the cultures, sort of like the pits. I couldn't tell her how I felt, though, because I didn't want her to know I was hiding out. That would have been like handing her a rope to tie me up with.

That girl can really roll. She tugged me along like I was a toy wagon. She only stopped once to look in a window at a pair of earings. Then she was off again. I swear Blackie knows the Spacer Sector better than I used to know Deadtown. Come to think of it, she also knows Deadtown better than me.

Medusa's isn't nearly as flashy as the human sector casinos. It doesn't have a lot of the games. There's roulette for the Lyrri, and a few numbers games. Out back there are the rat fights. Blackie was headed for the restaurant, with its big bar next door. She insisted on taking a table where everyone could see her. I don't know if she cared about seeing them.

I was scoping like mad, but not picking up any danger signals. At least, not the ones I was looking for. Chaz wasn't anywhere around, though I saw some people who could have been his relatives. No, something else was wrong. Something political.

I wonder if it was because of the raid at the Baby School. That was a human-owned, human-staffed business, and I'm sure lots of humans are pissed that the Q'rin stepped into their territory and basically pissed on it. I'd like to think they're mad because of the children, but I just didn't scope that.

Anyway, all the Q'rin were mostly on one side of the room and all the humans on another. Some Aesopians were sitting closer to the Q'rin, but not exactly with them. The Lyrri sat all over, like they didn't give a shit. Some were even sitting with Q'rin, which was weird. The Q'rin hate the Lyrri. But I suppose some associations transcend politics. Blackie and I sat there in the middle, like idiots, with menus in our hands.

"You notice anything wrong?" I asked her.

"Just ignore it!" she snapped, before I could finish speaking. Maybe she thought she could make it all go away by hiding in that menu.

It was a lot like the fast-food stalls before the fight. Maybe not quite so volatile, because there were so many dogs in the restaurant wearing force guns. I watched the government workers at the next table—two men in cheap glo-suits. I swear, that's where the kids get their lousy taste.

"Rich bastards say they've got everything under control," the bald one said as he sneaked looks at Blackie out of the corner of his eye. "Can't even control their own dogs. They're getting too big for their britches."

"So what do you want?" the other guy said. "You want the Q'rin to take over? You gotta give something up to get something."

Blackie had put her menu down and was flicking her eyes back and forth across the room. They were too bright. The smile was in place. A waiter came over to take our orders, and when he got away again he looked rumpled and exhausted.

"What's up?" I asked her.

"Why do you always have to be so suspicious?"

I think she was getting ready to wet her pants. I made the fatal mistake of trying to scope through her static and got a blinding headache for my trouble. The waiter came back with the three drinks she had ordered for herself and got away as quickly as he could.

"You'll feel better after you eat something," I said, watching her drain the last one.

"You just don't know what it's like."

"Huh?"

She twitched the smile into a grimace and back again.

"People are always wanting something from me. It's like the people in the casino, you know? First they like me and then they hate me."

"You mean the people you were hanging all over?"

She socked me in the arm, smiling with her teeth now. "I swear, Shade. Sometimes you can be such a fucking bitch. Just—really."

I was beginning to wonder if it was worth it to hang around for lunch. The food came before I could make up my mind. She picked at hers the way she always does, afraid to show her appetite. I ate like a pig.

"I just hate it when people hate me," she said.

"Don't worry about what other people think."

"I do worry."

"Then start worrying about what I think, because I'm sick of this shit."

She got very, very quiet, so I looked up. She looked like I had slapped her in the face. Her lip was trembling. I turned back to my lunch and ignored her until she got herself under control. I had about twenty minutes of blessed quiet. I knew I had opened the rift between us even wider.

When I looked up again the mask was in place. She was making eyes at some Lyrri-dog. My blood froze.

"Stop it," I said.

She acted like she didn't hear me. The Lyrri smiled back at her, gently.

"Aren't they just the sexiest things in the galaxy?" she whispered.

"No."

"I mean, like porcelain angels. Not an ounce of fat anywhere on their bodies."

"You can't even tell the men from the women," I said, which was dumb, because Blackie couldn't care less about that.

"Look," I said. "I've got some errands to run. I'll see you later."

I got up and left some credits on the table. She gave me a hurt little girl look. Was it for my benefit or the Lyrri's? He was getting ready to come over any minute.

"Just stay calm," I told her. It was an old

password between us. It means everything's sort
of okay.

I left just as he came over to the table. I glanced
back and saw her sitting with her shoulders
slumped. The Lyrri had an—I don't know—*abstract*
look on his face. It was weird.

I went out the rear exit. Blackie wouldn't try
to follow me out there because of the rats, which
are as big as canines. I heard their hissing and
the lashing of their tails even before I got outside.

Fortunately, the crowds obscured what was
going on in the rat-pits. The bettors didn't seem
to give a shit about racial tensions while the rats
were fighting. They stood shoulder to shoulder
and spoke their own special language. I slipped
past them as quickly as I could, toward the alley.
I was almost there when I caught a glimpse of
Snag. He was just disappearing around the corner.

Snag would rather eat rats than watch them
fight. What was he doing there?

I ran after him, and saw him just as he turned
another corner. He never looked over his shoulder, but he was moving fast, so I had to work to
keep up. Almost lost him as he hopped a tran.
I got on the one just behind it and kept a close
watch out the window.

For once I didn't pay any attention to the people in my own vicinity. Chaz himself could have
gotten on that tran with me, and I wouldn't have
known it. We rode the Eastern line, cutting across
the edges of the Spacer Sector and Deadtown
(where the drivers let people off but don't let
anyone on), then straight into Midtown. I could
see Snag's head bobbing back and forth in the
window, but he didn't move other than than
that.

After a while I realized we were probably going to ride to the end of the line before he made his move. I settled in to wait. I felt hands fumbling for my money stash (or just fumbling) from time to time, but I just slapped at them. Finally, we reached the end of the line, and I saw Snag get up to leave. He was the last one on his tran, and when I looked up I saw I was the last one on mine, too. I jumped out the door just as he was about to disappear, and then it was follow-the-leader again.

That far out in Capital are mostly city utilities and warehouses. A few guards, but hardly anything else. He was moving slower now, and was glancing over his shoulder from time to time. Almost caught me twice.

He was headed straight for Smoke River. I felt stupid for following him. He loves to go out there and lie on the river bottom. I had better things to do.

But something was up—I could scope it. I wondered if Knossos was hiding out there. My heart beat faster at the thought.

Snag's big feet went slap-slap in the mud, so I didn't worry too much about making noise. Instead I concentrated on not losing sight of him in the mist that floated over the river. The mist is from all the chemicals they dump in there. Snag must have a hide of steel—maybe he even likes the stuff.

He was moving toward a big shape on the shore. As I watched, the shape moved. The mist parted for a second and I saw an elephant man.

I almost yelled.

But it wasn't Knossos. I couldn't see him that well, but I could feel it. Snag walked up to him and they talked too low for me to hear. I squatted down behind some stinky plants.

Snag went into the river. The elephant man stood and waited on the bank. Sometimes he looked around, but mostly he just stared at the water. I tried not to swat the bugs that flew into my face. If I hadn't had such confidence in the rat hunters, I would have been looking out for rats, too. Before rat-fights got popular, rats used to be a real terror out here. A pack of them could kill you in half a minute. Now they keep to the deep swamps.

Finally the elephant man bent toward the water and grabbed something. He pulled a big box ashore, with poor Snag hanging on the other end of it like a wet noodle. Snag sat on the bank, and the elephant man heaved the box up on his shoulders. They talked a bit more, and then the elephant man trudged off toward the marsh, away from the city.

Snag rested a little longer before he headed back to the Outskirts. I followed him. We were almost back to the transport when suddenly he stiffened. I ducked out of sight.

"Mind your own bizznezz, little girl!" he yelled.

I waited a few minutes before I peeked. He was gone.

Blackie was still out when I got back. Jake was sitting drunk in the middle of the living room, an ugly look on his face. I went upstairs and found Farouk sitting in the corner, his face the color of ashes.

"What's up?" I asked.

"Nothin'."

His brown eyes looked black. They seemed to have sunk farther into his head.

"You go to the stalls today?" I asked.

"Yeah." It was barely a whisper.

"What's happening out there these days?"

"Tinkers acting tough," he said. He looked me in the eye and I scoped him. My butt tightened up with the fear I felt there. "Seems like all people want to do is buy my ass," he said, which explained the physical reaction I got.

I pulled out some loki. "Have a smoke," I said.

He accepted it, but didn't unfold from his crouch.

"It's because the Babies are dead," I said.

"What's that supposed to mean?"

"There's less Baby ass to fill the demand. So now the customers have to look harder for it. It's at a premium. Chicken hawks have to hustle to find what's in demand, and the regular houses do too. They'll kidnap you if you don't want to go willingly, so watch out."

"No one is going to fuck my ass," he said.

"Good."

We smoked two sticks, but he just got tighter and tighter. "Came here with my uncle," he said. "He had a job, but he didn't last. Died without caring what happened to me."

There wasn't anything to say about that. I didn't think he wanted an answer anyway.

"When I get to be a man I'm going to beat some ass. You better believe it."

"Do that."

"I will." He closed his eyes and let his head fall against the wall. "Maybe I'll fuck some ass too. Some Baby ass."

"Think you'd like that?"

"*They* do. All of 'em do."

"Men?"

"Yeah. My uncle did. He never did it to me, but I knew what he was doing with older boys. Once he told me, 'It don't matter what they say on the vids and in books and stuff. They try to tell you men just like women. But that's bullshit. You'll never know what it's all about until you poke some nice, young—' "

He clenched his face up real tight and let it go again. "He never did me because he said that was incest. But he looked at me a lot. And *they* look at me a lot. So I wonder if he was right."

"How could he know what you would be like?" I asked. "People who're obsessed don't ever see outside their own lives."

"Obsessed?"

"Yeah. There're men who come all the way out to this sleazy zit of a planet to get a taste of what they know is impossible at home. They spend all their money on it. So you and I see a lot more of it than people do on, say, Earth. Now you're seeing it all the time, so you think it's normal. But only you are gonna know how you really feel about sex."

He nodded, even seemed comforted by that idea. It worried me a little. Don't want him getting the notion I have all the answers. I just felt bad for him is all.

"How come you're not a Deadtowner anymore?" he asked finally.

"What do you think a Deadtowner is?"

He sighed. "You don't let 'em fuck your ass. You take what you need."

"That's me," I said.

"I don't know."

"I don't have to convince you."

I got up and went to the bathroom. When I came back he was crying.

"I'm sick of not knowing what's gonna happen next," he said.

I squatted next to him. "Look," I said, "one thing I can tell you for sure. Stealing is better than selling your ass. Pimps and chicken hawks take all your money. You get food, clothing, a place to sleep, but nothing else. A Deadtowner learns how to sleep on a stone bed and eat whatever happens by. It's not easy, but it's better. Believe me."

I went downstairs to let him cry alone. Right now he's talking in his sleep. I didn't bring this notebook out until he stopped thrashing around.

Blackie and Jake fought for three hours when she came home. That's okay with me. Kept her from asking me how I got her fancy clothes all muddy.

Maybe it's not exactly fair for me to say it's better to be a Deadtowner than a Baby or a whore. I believe it, but when I follow my argument to its inevitable end, I have to admit that's like saying Deadtowners are better than prostitutes. That's the same kind of attitude I hear every day from toughs in rag-wraps who don't know what it's like to be beaten to a pulp every time you try to fight. It's the same attitude that got me into the fight with that tinker. Because he thought he was better than me.

But I do believe what I told Farouk.

At the same time, I don't blame the prostitutes. Especially the Babies, who are used to being taken care of. From what some of them have told me, the sex was happening to them even before they left home. And maybe living at the Baby School was less confusing to them than the streets.

I think some of them have even learned to mistake sex for affection. A lot of them learn to crave it. After all, human beings are tactile, sexual creatures. But it makes me sick when I hear self-serving pedophiles saying that what they do is okay because the kids want it. Like they're doing some kind of service to the lonely, sex-starved children of the galaxy. Makes me violent if I listen to it for too long.

Anyway, I was shocked when I realized what the Baby School really was. I had been living like a Skid, eating at the Salvation Army with Knossos and the others. I guess I still entertained ideas of getting off-planet, so I wandered around the city looking for an exit and digging in the trash.

Once I saw some kids talking to some tinkers. After awhile, some of the kids went off with them. I went back to digging in the garbage and didn't think anything more about it.

Then I heard this squeaky voice say, "Hi!"

I looked up. A little girl was tugging on my jacket and smiling at me.

"What's up?" I asked her. She looked healthy and clean. Looked about seven. I was sure her mother would come get her any moment.

"I'm Ramona!" she said, like it was the most wonderful news in the world. "What's your name?"

"Shade," I said, proud of that if nothing else.

"How come you're doing *that*?" she asked.

"Because I'm hungry."

"I know where you can get some food," she said.

Something made the hair on the back of my neck stand up. I looked at her again, and this time I scoped her.

If I didn't know people like Mira and Knossos, it would be easy to hate the universe.

"No thanks," I said.

Her face crumpled. "But it's real nice!"

"No."

"Please?"

She wasn't trying to recruit me. Ramona, despite her circumstances, was a loving child. She liked me at first sight and wanted me to come home with her.

"Look," I said. "I'm hungry, but I don't want to fuck men just so I can eat."

She thought about this for a moment. "Eddie goes out at four o'clock. If you come, I won't tell anyone you stole."

It was tantalizing.

"I'll come and look, okay?"

She smiled and led me back to the kids on the corner. They looked at me curiously. The older ones smirked as if they thought they knew something I didn't—which they did—but they weren't hostile like the adult hookers. Babies work for room, board, and baubles. And they're happier together than they are alone.

And in case any of you thinks that what passes for a government on Z'taruh cares about the way these kids are exploited, think again. Children are not allowed to own property or have bank accounts here. You can be sure that the people who are responsible for making up that law have their hands in the Baby-ass till. Not to mention other parts of their anatomy.

Ramona took me to an ugly, cheap building a couple of blocks away. It was in that area of Midtown between Deadtown and the Spacer Sector. I figured it was an apartment building. She took me around to one of the bolt-holes. It was a hole in the floor of the next building that led to a sub-basement, which led to a crawlspace, which led to a closet that opened into the dorm.

I stepped out into a Baby whorehouse. Later I found out that the Baby School was the biggest whorehouse in Capital. There were some smaller ones, but the Q'rin-dogs kept cleaning those out. They raided the Baby School from time to time, but never like they did this last time. I got the feeling some rich guy up on the Hill was paying the dogs off.

Guess that fell through.

"Who's this Eddie guy?" I asked Ramona.

"Babysitter," she said as she led me into the kitchen.

It was the first of many stolen meals at the Baby School. Also the first time I saw a Scarbaby. He had burns all over his back and arms.

"What happened to him?" I asked Ramona.

"He was bad, so—so they make him lie down and make him take off his clothes—"

"Who does? Eddie?"

"No. The men come, and Eddie says, 'You want chicken or a Scarbaby?' And mostly they want to fuck, but sometimes they want a Scarbaby."

The Scarbaby looked at me with contempt-filled eyes and left the room. A few weeks later he was dead. Most of them don't last more than a few months. Except for Stone, who lasted three years. Maybe he was just lucky, because they all seemed pretty expert at what they did.

Maybe *lucky* is a lousy choice of words.

Eddie stayed away for three hours. The chicken hawks would never give their Babies that much freedom, but management was lousy at the Baby School. I heard there were lots of partners in the business. I only ever saw the lackeys; they were mean but stupid bastards. Eddie wasn't any better or worse than ol' Larry. Those kids mostly took care of themselves, and they were pretty good at it.

Once Blackie told me she knew who really owned the Baby School. She said it was definitely someone on the Hill. If I had asked her who it was, she probably would have told me, but I didn't want to know. I'm not sure why. Whoever it is, they didn't involve themselves in anything but the profit end of things, I bet. They didn't worry about how things were run unless the profit margin went down.

I guess it's at zero right now. They probably cut their losses and went on to the next venture.

In fact, maybe the raid was their way of doing just that.

The people on the Hill think they're better. Maybe they use the same argument I do. Or maybe, like most rich people, they believe poor people wouldn't know what to do with money if they had it. I know what I'd do with mine. I wonder what Knossos is doing with his.

I keep thinking about that box Snag brought up from Smoke River. I think it was big enough to hold force rifles.

I went to the Salvation Army for breakfast this morning. Raided Blackie's dressing room and came up with a poor-kid look that I figured wouldn't draw attention.

No one I knew was there. Not Mira or Snag or especially Knossos. Not even any of the people I just knew slightly. It really cut me off at the knees. Now I had a whole day to kill.

I decided to go back to Blackie's and see if Farouk wanted to spend the day with me. I even considered asking Blackie, which shows you how desperate I was. I was walking past the alley behind the S.A. when a huge hand reached out of the darkness and touched my shoulder.

It was Knossos.

"Jesus!" I blurted, "Where have you been? I've been looking all over for you!"

"Step into the alley," he said.

I did, and we both drew back out of sight. "I'm sorry," I said. "But where have you been?"

"I can't tell you that," he said. His face was even more unreadable than usual, but the way he was standing made me feel that he must be tired— something rare for an elephant man. "I need your help," he said.

"You've got it. You need to make some money again?"

"Yes, but not at the pits. I can't be seen there anymore."

No stupid questions, Shade. But oh, how I wanted to ask them. "How about poker?" I said.

"That was my thought, too. It would be best if we stuck to the human sector. I'll defer to your judgement in the choice of location and players."

"Right," I said. "I know exactly where to go."

I was thinking of the hotel where Conners and I had played back when I got my butt marooned on this planet. It was a second-rate place, and no one there would blink twice at Knossos's apparent lack of money.

"Ah—listen," I said. "I never tried to hide an elephant man before—"

"Leave that to me," he said. "Just tell me where you think we should go, and I will get us there unseen."

So I did, and true to his word, he moved like he was on reconnaissance back on Ragnir. He took me through alleys and back ways I didn't even know about—but then, I never needed to hide myself the way he apparently has. Not until lately, anyway. I took careful note of our route, for future reference.

Took us about half an hour to get to the section of the Spacer Sector I wanted, and then we headed straight for the hotel, only slipping back into hiding twice at the glimpse of Q'rin-dogs. The first time it happened, Knossos told me, "If we're spotted, run away as fast as you can. I'll cover you."

"Things are that bad, huh?"

"Yes," he said, already moving off again.

The Star Lodge no longer looked glitzy to me. The sign out front was missing, and the inside had turned rather seedy. But it was comfortable and long on the features that really count, like good booze (for those who care) and quiet rooms in which to play poker. Knossos and I went straight to the bar. We caused a minor sensation there; not so much because Knossos is an Aesopian, but because he's so big. The waitress had to search to find a chair large enough to come close to accommodating him.

"We don't often get people your size in here," she apologized.

"Perhaps that will change," said Knossos.

"I hope so!" she said brightly, and ran off to fetch our drinks.

Knossos was silent for a long time after she had come and gone again, leaving me a beer and him a whiskey. "Anything wrong?" I asked him.

"I was just thinking of the House of Voices, back Home," he said. "Specifically, of my seat there. I can imagine it gathering dust without me."

"No one else would sit there while you're away?"

He turned grim eyes in my direction. "No one. Not until my death."

"Well, that won't be for a long time." I guzzled the first half of my beer to that thought. He saluted me with his.

"The same for you, Shade. And longer."

We were already getting looks from the poker hopefuls, and before long four of them wandered over. "Mind if we join you?" one guy asked in a slightly exaggerated Earth Southern drawl. He became Mr. South for me.

"Please do," Knossos said graciously.

Mr. South and his friends sat down. He did the talking while the other three checked us out.

"We're in town for a few days on business. Insurance, not that I'm making a pitch."

"Of course not," said Knossos. "I expect you must be very tired of talking about premiums. All work and no play, as the saying goes—"

"You said it, friend," said Mr. South.

"Now my friend and I," Knossos indicated me, "were hoping we could find someone interested in playing cards with us. I hope you don't mind my being blunt, but I sense you're interested in the same thing."

"You have good senses. I like a man who comes to the point. Do you have a room here?"

His eyes must have told him that we didn't have a room anywhere, but he didn't show it. I liked him for that.

"No," said Knossos. "You?"

"Room 812. See you there in fifteen minutes?"

"Agreed."

So off they went to their rooms. We stayed put for a few minutes to plot strategy.

"Are you sure you need me?" I asked him. "You seem to be doing pretty darn well on your own."

"In such matters it is always best to have an ally," Knossos said. "Together we are formidable, don't you agree?"

"Yes," I said, torn between greed and pride.

Knossos stood and made his kingly way to the elevator, with me trailing along behind. "Come again!" the waitress called to us. I was glad we had left her a good tip.

"These guys are straightforward," I was telling Knossos. "So we can play a regular game. No nonsense, no cheating to watch out for."

He nodded. I taught Knossos to play poker myself, and I wasn't worried that he couldn't handle anything that came along. He has the best poker face I've ever seen, and he's got natural talent.

As we were riding up to our floor, I was thinking how strange it was to run into Knossos after looking for him so long. It felt good to be with him again, but it also felt so natural that I couldn't be excited about it. He and I were going to beat the pants off these guys, and were going to do it by playing fair. That was what he wanted. He patted me on the shoulder as if he sensed what I was thinking. "I know we'll do well," he said.

As we stepped into the dim hallway I thought, *Wouldn't it be funny, what with the way I've run into Knossos today, if I ran into Chaz, too?* It didn't seem likely, since the only other person in the hall was a huge human, a guy almost as big as Knossos. He was walking toward us and giving me the twice-over. To make matters worse, he was talking to himself.

"What do you mean the price has gone up?" he said. "We've got three days to go at Packrat's Plot just to pay the bills, and you come up with this crap about reduced supply! You'll sell me three crates of lizards at the standard rate, or you'll have Fauna Control up your asses so fast—!"

Knossos was ignoring him. I slipped behind the elephant man to get out of sight to those baleful eyes.

"I'm sick of the way you little bastards keep trying to cheat me," Mr. Huge continued. "You think I won't go to the law? I can get immunity as an informant, and you can get ten years on Odin for selling a protected life form. Especially— heh, heh—considering what happens to the poor little things after you sell 'em to me. Understand?"

Knossos and this guy had to squeeze around each other as they met in the hall. I glued myself to Knossos's back to avoid contact with the man, and Knossos did his best to accommodate me.

"Yes," I heard a soft, familiar voice say, "I think we understand each other perfectly." And as the big guy moved past us, we caught sight of the man behind him, someone we couldn't have seen until that moment.

It was Chaz. I must be a precog or something.

Chaz and Knossos went icy cold when they saw each other, and I got a good look at the bone-deep hatred their two races feel for each other. The Aesopians are the only people in the galaxy the Lyrri actually fear. Chaz was pressed as far against the wall as he could go, just like I was. And let me tell you, it was gratifying to see that. Nice to know he could feel that way too.

He didn't recognize me. I think it was a combination of my disguise and his preoccupation with Knossos. Chaz and the big guy went to their room and we went to ours, and the incident seemed practically forgotten. Evidently we all had business to attend to. But I made a note of which room they went into. Now I wish I hadn't.

Anyway, the guys were waiting for us. My estimation of their abilities rose considerably as we entered the room. They looked polite, friendly, relaxed. But they were awed by Knossos's presence in that small room, and they had gone to the trouble to procure a large, reinforced stool for his considerable mass. They had whiskey on one of the dressers, but just enough for socializing. No one was planning to get drunk.

"Why don't you have a seat here?" Mr. South asked, indicating that I should sit on his right. That put him between Knossos and me, which was okay.

"All right," I said, hoping the other three would do something to individualize themselves for me. They still seemed too much alike. Another sign of their skill. Players that good don't need to cheat.

"We were thinking to start with Five Card Stud," said Mr. South.

Knossos nodded, and I said "Okay." I didn't have to pretend I didn't care. One game is as good as another to me. Like I've said before, the effort is in trying not to win too much, even when I'm playing fair. As it turned out, for this game I didn't have to work as hard to make it look good, and I was glad Knossos was there to complicate things.

I studied the other three guys, and for the time being decided to name them Number One, Number Two, and Number Three. We all pulled out wads of credit—I still had plenty left over from my adventure at the pits with Mira—and I could see that we were going to end up with no-limit poker, no matter how we started out.

Mr. South dealt the first hand, and he also won it with a straight flush. Knossos won the next two, then I won two after that, and then we switched to Seven Card Stud.

Along about that time, I noticed something about Number Two. Once he was dealt his cards he always looked at everyone with this "What Have You Got" expression on his face. Nothing else. I started to think of him as Mr. Curious, then eventually switched to Mr. Eyebrows. That shows you how tough this sessions was, because usually I've got everyone pegged immediately. After me and Knossos and Mr. South, he was the best player, with Numbers One and Three tying for last place. But those rankings were pretty close, and eventually all we were doing was moving money back and forth between us. We played most of the games known to us, plus variations of same, until finally Mr. South said, "Say. Let's stop messing around and get down to serious business. You all ever heard of Texas Hold 'Em?"

Knossos sighed with satisfaction. "My favorite game," he said. "And, as in war, the limits should be very high."

The energy level in the room jumped drastically. Knossos was right to compare Texas Hold 'Em to war. Or to business, or life, or anything else that's dangerous and wildly unpredictable. I've known lots of players who refused to touch it. But it was Knossos's strongest game. And mine. The thought made me a little uncomfortable.

Anyway, at this point I knew there were only one or two games left in this session to decide who was going to take home the money.

"Exactly what limit are we talking about here?" Number One asked.

"Five hundred thousand credits," Knossos said.

"Well, that would do it," said Number Three, meaning that would clean him out. Or any of us.

What makes Texas Hold 'Em so interesting is that after two cards are dealt to each player, face down, and the guy to the left of the dealer bets, and everyone either sees that bet or raises it, three more communal cards are placed in the center of the table face up. Anyone can use them to strengthen their hands. More betting takes place, but this time the players can check. Then two more cards are dealt face up, one at a time, with a round of betting after each. You have to have nerve. And money. Numbers One and Three lost all theirs after the first hand. Knossos won that one.

He was playing on his own by now, and I was just trying to stay out of his way. I figured we'd get rid of Mr. Eyebrows first, which we did, and then either Knossos or I would take a bow and the other would take out Mr. South. I was getting ready to leave the two of them to it when Mr. South suddenly folded after the fourth round.

"Sorry folks," he said, "but I've got to have

something to get home on. The wife'll kill me if she has to bail me out again."

Knossos and I looked at each other. I was wishing Mr. South hadn't said that bit about getting home, because suddenly I was very aware of the money in the pot for its own sake. There was enough on the table to buy me I.D. and get me off the planet, maybe even back to Earth if I planned properly. Or there was enough to get Knossos out from under the debt that had kept him stranded on Z'taruh for so many years. I could see it in his eyes, the weight of all those people who had served under him and still depended on him to lead them *somewhere,* and the pain he felt for making them wait so long.

What I couldn't see was if there was a place in it for me anywhere. And I wanted it so bad—to be part of his plan, to be with Lord Knossos and see Home.

But he hadn't asked me. And I had to take care of myself. He had already won twice what he had brought with him, even without this pot. And I had a feeling that my Four of a Kind beat whatever he could make out of his hand.

"I'll raise you a thousand," I said.

He just stared at me with those old eyes that held no anger, or resentment, or accusation—only respect.

"You are a worthy opponent," he said.

I rested my arms on the table so my hands wouldn't shake.

"I fold," he said, and put his cards down without turning them over. I did the same.

I gathered up my winnings, and Knossos and I stood to leave.

"You are good players," he told the men.

From anyone else it might have sounded sarcastic, but they took it as the praise it really was.

"Mister, I can't say I ever enjoy losing money," Mr. South drawled, "but it surely was a pleasure meeting you." He saluted Knossos with the drink. "And an honor."

As we were about to leave, Number One rushed forward. "Wait," he said.

Knossos turned to face him.

"I just wanted to tell you—I served on Ragnir. Near the end of the war. I was just a kid. I served under Lord Ashraan. I stayed 'til the end, even after the recall. *I stayed*."

Knossos looked at him for a moment, then extended his huge hand. The two of them shook.

We left them, closing the door behind us, and walked down the hall. The door to Chaz's room stood open. It was dead quiet in there. Knossos and I got on the elevator.

We had only gone down a couple of floors when I pushed the STOP button.

"Look," I said. "I want you to have this money. Please take it."

I didn't look at him, because I was afraid I would cry or something stupid like that.

"If that is your wish," he said, "I'll accept the money."

"It is."

He put his hands on my shoulders and I felt a warmth like the memory of my father rocking me to sleep. I looked up and saw a tear rolling down his face. It disappeared in the deep lines on his cheeks.

"Shade," he said, "I grieve for the children at the Baby School."

"Yeah." I let out a deep breath. "Me too."

"Don't hate all Q'rin because of what a few have done."

"That's a strange thing for an Aesopian to say. Especially you."

"Listen." He gave me a slight shake. "Whether someone is your friend or your enemy does not depend on the shape of his body or the place he was born."

"All right," I said. "I know."

And I did. Wasn't I standing there with the elephant man, respecting him more than I did myself and wishing I could follow him back into hiding?

He let go of my shoulders.

"Just tell me one thing," I said. "What is your debt?"

He shook his massive head. "I can't tell you. But I can tell you to whom it is owed."

"Good enough."

"The Q'rin never took Home. Not even after they had defeated us everywhere else. We would have destroyed it before we let them take it; and there are those among the Q'rin who value Home almost as much as we do."

I had only seen it in a dream, but I believed.

"Those of us who were Out could not go Home. We had run out of money. The Q'rin confiscated our assets, and we had to pay to get them back."

So they had his ship. I nodded and kept my big mouth shut.

"There are other ways we could have reclaimed those assets, from Q'rin who are willing to sponsor us. But I choose not to have a master. And there are those who will prevent me from paying my debt, if they can."

"I understand."

"Good," he said. "Now understand this. If you tell anyone that you have seen me, or that you have helped me in any way, the Q'rin will execute you. I will not have you pay that price for me. Don't be like the Babies, Shade."

"I won't," I promised.

I gave him his money, and pushed the LOBBY button. The elevator lurched back into motion.

Knossos pushed the TWO button. "We should leave separately," he said.

"Right."

When we got to his floor and the door opened, he hesitated. His eyes seemed to ask, "Will you be all right?"

"I'll be fine," I said.

"Take care," he told me, and the doors shut him away from me.

I stood there and wondered if I would ever see him again.

When I got down to the lobby, I saw Chaz walking out of the bar. I held the elevator door and watched him leave the hotel.

Where was Mr. Huge?

I don't know why I gave a damn, but I went back up to the eighth floor. The door to Chaz's room still stood open.

It was like one of those stupid vids where you yell, "Don't go in there" at the screen, but the dumb fool goes in anyway. My legs moved me forward, and I could almost hear the let's-build-the-tension music in my ears. I looked through the open doorway.

The big guy's blood painted the walls and the floor. It must have taken him awhile to die. He was propped in the corner with about twenty or thirty knives in him. Lord only knows where Chaz had gotten them—maybe they were already in the room. I'd hate to think he could hide that many knives under his clothes.

Mr. Huge had a surprised look on his face, like he couldn't believe a skinny little Lyrri could hurt him like that. I guess their *business* must have gone bad.

I turned my back on the sight and went back to the elevator. I rode down to the lobby and strolled out of the hotel. Once I was sure Chaz wasn't around, I ran all the way back to Blackie's place.

When I got back to Blackie's, Farouk wasn't there.

Lately I get the feeling that the people I thought I knew never really existed.

Blackie was awake by then. She shook her head over what I was wearing and insisted on making me over. I felt strangely relieved to have something to do, even if it was just to sit and be prodded and hassled. I tried to listen to what she was saying, but most of it went right past me.

Then I heard, ". . . can't believe they actually invited me. It must have been my aunt Nikki, because—like—she's a free spirit too and just, you know, always understood me. Do you think I should go?"

"Will there be free food?"

"Tons."

"Will you take me with you?"

She yanked at my wig, pulling it over my right ear. "You dipshit! I'm serious!" she said.

"So am I!"

"Really? Seriously?"

"Yes! I'm bored out of my skull. Where is this

thing being held?" (I still wasn't sure what we were talking about.)

"My parent's house."

Ah hah! No ties, huh?

"Well shit, Blackie! I'd think you'd want some company. You could pass me off as one of your rich friends. We could eat all the great food and watch the freaks."

"I don't know. It's just—those people are really boring."

"Maybe to you. I've never seen any of those fancy houses from the inside. Look, if it gets too weird we'll just leave early. Come on."

Silence from Blackie.

"When is it?"

"Tomorrow," she said, like she thought that might change my mind.

"All right."

She sighed. "You'd just better not think I'm a rich bitch. I mean it, Shade. I don't live there anymore."

"I know."

"I mean it!"

"I know!"

Now it's late and Farouk still hasn't come home. Maybe he's trying to wean himself away from this place. At least I know he's not at the Baby School, for what that's worth.

I thought Blackie would never get up this morning. Actually, I didn't see her face until late afternoon. She looked surly and hungover, snapped at everything I said, and seemed perfectly willing to forget all about tonight's party. But I wouldn't let her. I got all washed up and then started to dress myself, until she was forced to intervene and save me from my own bad taste. Eventually she perked up, but that might have had something to do with the stims she had with breakfast.

It was dark by the time we hopped a transport and headed up the hill. We were the last passengers aboard when we got to the end of the line.

I swear, up there even the air smells richer. I'd forgotten what streets look like when the trash is picked up regularly and the very road itself gets scrubbed. Landscaping and sparkling walls on every side. Even the best streets in Beverly Hills never looked this good. Blackie acted like she didn't even notice the difference.

"My parents might not let me in," she said. "So—like—don't get too disappointed if they get mad, okay?"

But when we got to her parents' house, she just charged up the front walk like she still lived there. No one looked twice at us. In fact, hardly anyone looked once.

I'm not sure what I expected from these people —maybe something like Petronius's *Satyricon*; you know, decadent rich people walking around half-naked and shitting in public. Or Supertech Executives, all eight feet tall, lean and shiny like machines. I was pretty disappointed with these Sunday brunch anal-retentive conservatives, who all stood around chatting quietly and looking vaguely annoyed. My mom would have had them completely out-classed.

Blackie disappeared immediately. I was at a loss until I remembered to scope. I had turned off to avoid Blackie's static, and wasn't getting any more information about what might happen than anyone else. I have to be more careful about that in the future.

Once I switched on, things looked very different.

Real power can't be observed the way you observe a rainstorm or some other natural phenomenon. You think the lightning is the power. But the trick is to see the lightning *before* it strikes. Or in this case, the piranha.

I moved toward the buffet before they could home in on me. You've got to keep moving in company like that. Blackie knew that, even if I'd forgotten it.

The food was incredible. I went through two plates in fifteen minutes and headed for the desert table. It featured fresh fruit, pastries, and a candy that's popular in the Spacer Sector right now—a chocolate and caramel thing coated with a mild halucinogen. I loaded up on the junk and ignored the healthy stuff.

"Wouldn't you rather have some fruit?" said a compact, pleasant-looking man in his late thirties. I scoped him and decided he was all right.

"No," I said.

"Well, me neither, really. But I think I'll stick with the pastries. Those Dreambars give me a headache."

He was one of those rare people who seems to be happy whether he's rich or poor. He reminded me of Mr. Greenteeth, or my Aunt Katie. I liked him and stayed near him most of the night.

But I was wondering. I used to play the Beverly Hills crowd pretty well. These people were sharper, but just as easily scoped. Over there were some casino owners. They were talking to a couple of swamp-farm kings, the drug lords of Z'taruh. And there was one guy who was a swamp-miner, a Big Boss who is using illegal labor to tap natural gasses (the planet is so full of gas they should have named it *Fart*).

Anyway, the casino guys have a Baby Ass habit, and the swamp-miner has a drug problem. The two drug lords have a collection of lesser problems that could be easily exploited.

And there were the developers. A lot of them were floating around. In fact, my friend the nice guy is one. His name is Mr. Field, and his work is fairly legit—upgrading the government buildings and building some of the prefab communities the workers live in. He's also done some work for the Q'rin; basically the same kind of thing.

"You seem like a smart girl," he said. "You still in school?"

"No."

"Come 'round to my office if you're looking for work," he said, handing me a card. "We'll test you and see what you're good at. I mean, you can't live off Mom and Dad forever, right?"

That was tactful. Somehow he knew I wasn't a rich kid. Maybe it was the way I had stuffed myself at the buffet. "I might do that," I said.

Most of the other developers were the build-em-and-run variety. They use the very cheapest materials, half the time not even bothering to finish what they start. They lure the tinkers in and drain them dry with fine-print taxes and deductions, and then get a kickback from the casinos, who have financed the whole deal to begin with. The drug lords have the same kind of arrangement with the developers. And everyone turns around and invests the money off-world—

which is where they raise the bonds to build in
the first place.

Mr. Field and I drifted from room to room,
looking at all the fancy furnishings and the neu-
rotic art. Blackie flitted past several times at the
speed of light. Once I noticed she was clutching
an ashtray.

"What do these people do for a living?" I asked
Mr. Field. "I mean the owners of this house."

He frowned. "I think they own property in the
Spacer Sector. I know they speculate in art. An-
tiques and modern stuff. I'm sure they have some
heavy duty investments, too."

"Oh." I was looking at some religious figurines
grouped in a corner with an expressionist painting that looked like bloody vomit. It left a bad
taste in my mouth, to say the least. "Do they
have any dealings with the Q'rin Lords?"

"No way." His tone of voice told me how much
he was understating that. All the people who
live on the hill are human, and it would seem
Blackie's parents are more human than most.
They didn't even invite any Lyrri to this party,
and I hear they're in vogue right now.

Mr. Field went over to talk to his wife, a pretty
woman who has aspirations in the art invest-
ment field. She was making a fuss over the stuff
in the house. Blackie's Mom was there too, watching everyone with her crazy eyes. I guess the art
thing is what her husband uses to keep her busy.

Too bad she doesn't have Blackie's static. Scoping her was like looking at the bloody-vomit painting. She and Blackie avoided each other like the
plague.

I drifted out toward the pool; didn't want to
wear out my welcome with Mr. Field. The pool

was fed by a waterfall and lined with black marble and lava. It was beautiful, but not inviting. People sat in little alcoves, talking and looking at the panoramic view of the city lights. You could even see the Q'rin sector from there. I sensed the darker current of business dealings out in the open air.

Someone offered me a tray of drinks. I took a plain fruit juice. Mr. Field had been right; the Dreambars were giving me a headache. The sound of the water was peaceful, even if the half-heard conversations weren't. I gazed at the view and wondered where out there Knossos might be. *Maybe he has his ship back by now.*

I felt someone checking me out. The feeling made me think of Lenny the Chicken Hawk. I looked sideways at the source and saw a man standing there with two other men. I scoped them, and was reminded of something that happened a few years ago in Beverly Hills.

In fact, it was at another party. One of my mother's friends invited me—but didn't invite my mother. Lots of kids were there, so I didn't think anything of it. I had slipped into the den to stuff my face in private when this so-called friend came in.

"Nice to get away from it all," he said.

"Oh yeah," I said, hoping he would go away.

"You sure have a healthy appetite."

"Oh well—" *chomp chomp chomp glom.* I thought maybe I could gross him out of the room.

"I hear you're a housekeeper," he said.

"Yeah."

"Make good money?"

"Yeah."

He laughed. "Bullshit. You don't know what money is."

"And you do," I said.

"That's right."

I shoved another eclair into my mouth.

"Well, then thanks for the free food, sucker," I said.

His eyes narrowed slightly. But he kept smiling.

"Sometimes I wonder if you kids really know how precious you are," he said.

"You mean valuable," I said, chewing with my mouth open.

"You're so healthy. I guess you don't know how obsessions can drive us adults."

"You're talking about kiddie porn, right? I know you're in the business. My mom doesn't. She thinks you sell insurance. I guess she thinks that's why no one can stand you."

"Are you gonna keep being smart with me, or do you wanna hear something maybe you didn't know?" he said.

"Quit bothering me."

"You're beautiful."

I laughed, spraying half-chewed eclair all over his expensive den. I was at the height of my fat, pimply faced years at the time, and I knew ugly when I saw it in the mirror. I wasn't the sort of girl who saw fat when there wasn't any, either. I was about one hundred and eighty-seven pounds. And I had enough zits to share with the whole free world. I just kept laughing at him as he played his feeble cards.

"I mean it," he said. "You teenaged girls are so desirable. You should take advantage of your opportunities while you can."

"Fuck off."

"Shit! You could retire at age twenty-five, girl! It just kills me to see young foxy ladies wasting their talents."

Something about the way he said *kills me* sent me a little off-balance. I knew what most men would say if they saw my overblown self on their vid screens while they were trying to jack off. It was the sort of thing that could put you off masturbation for life. So what else could they possibly want with me?

Maybe to see me tortured. Murdered. All customers demand for that kind of consumption is flesh. It doesn't have to be lean.

"Bondage is where the real money is," he said. "I mean, it's just special effects. They don't even tie the ropes tight—you could slip right out of them."

Money kept him from getting caught after I copped on him. And connections. On Z'taruh you don't even need that. Tonight these three men looked like they knew they could drag me out of there kicking and screaming without disturbing a soul. Bastards weren't even carrying weapons.

"Hi there," I said. "Nice party."

"Thank you," the first guy said. "I'm glad you could come."

Blackie's dad.

"Actually, your daughter Blackie invited me."

Didn't faze him. He doesn't feel anything for his wife and daughters. If he were hungry, he could eat them up and shit them out again without the slightest strain.

He just kept looking. Made me madder and madder. I took a few steps closer.

"Ever go to the pit fights?" I asked him.

He frowned at that. Xenophobia glowed in his eyes like a fever. "Hell, no," he said. He stepped closer too, leaving his weak friends behind. "I wouldn't soil my shoes."

"Don't worry too much about soiling your hands, do you?"

He grinned at me.

Before this I probably could have gone back inside and he would have forgotten about me before the night was up. But not now.

"I'll bet you've never even been to Deadtown," I said.

"Owned some property there," he answered.

I looked and looked, my eyes getting big behind my shades. My heart was pounding. Something shot up my throat and splattered all over his shoes. I heaved three more times while he back-pedaled.

"Thanks—had a nice time," I said, and ran away from there.

"I told you to watch out for those Dreambars!" Mr. Field said as I ran through the house.

I grabbed Blackie and told her it was time to go.

"Good," she said, and was out the door before I could blink twice.

On the way back to the transport I said, "So when you told me you knew who owned the Baby School you were talking about your dad, right?"

"Does it matter?"

"Fuck, yes."

"Please don't hate me because you hate him."

I could go for that. I wasn't feeling mad or sick at the moment. Just glad to get out of there, like a drowning person is glad to get her head above the water. A lot of details were coming together in my head. Blackie seemed calm. And after seeing what her dad thinks of her, I guess I was feeling sorrier for her than I ever had.

"Did you eat his food when you knew where it came from?" I asked.

"Yes."

"Well, you don't live there anymore, so what the fuck do I care?"

"It's like, all they seem to care about is money. And all my mom can talk about is how I'm not getting any younger and how I should get married while I still have my looks. How I'm wasting my life and not going to school and . . ."

She went on for a while. I heard some of it while I had thoughts about bloody-vomit paintings, vomit on expensive shoes. I don't think she said anything about Babies murdered while they slept because her father had a feud going with the Q'rin Lords. Finally she stopped and waited for me to comment.

"What does your mom mean 'you're not getting any younger'?" I asked.

"I'm twenty-five."

I couldn't believe that. She laughed at the look on my face.

"How old did you think I was?" she asked.

"Eighteen. Nineteen."

She hugged me like it was some big compliment. It wasn't. Arrested development isn't anything to be proud of.

"Does your mom do drugs or something? She looked pretty dazed."

"She smokes and drinks like you wouldn't believe. And she loves stims. Sometimes she stays

awake for days, you know? And it's like—we tell
her to quit, but she just keeps doing it."

Sounded like Blackie's very own life.

"How about your dad?"

No answer.

"How long has he been feuding with the Q'rin
Lords?"

"Forever, I guess. He hated having to pay them
protection money for the Baby School. Don't talk
about that now, okay? Talking about bad stuff is
like—just—attracting bad luck."

Didn't matter anyway. It all made sense now.
The Q'rin had wiped out Blackie's dad's stock.
And now he's scouting around for snuff-vid ma-
terial to make up for his losses.

We waited for the transport without talking,
and kept the silence all the way home. When we
got back to Blackie's place she started to unload
her inner pockets. Ashtrays, silverware, jewelry,
and just plain junk. She had this satisfied look
on her face.

I went upstairs. Farouk was still gone. I came
back down and watched Blackie. She was ar-
ranging and rearranging the stuff, really concen-
trating on her work.

"Have you seen Farouk lately?" I asked.

"No."

"He hasn't come back two nights in a row
now."

Blackie turned so I couldn't see her face and
kept fussing with the junk.

"You think Jake has seen him?" I asked.

"You should ask him, because they always hang
around together."

"So where's Jake?"

She straightened up and threw an ashtray at the wall. "Fucking piece of shit!"

"Who? Jake?"

She looked at me. "I remember now. Farouk said he was moving out."

"You remember now."

"God, Shade! Just—" she pulled out a cigarette and fell onto the couch. "I'm treading water as fast as I can."

I had a real headache. "Thanks for taking me to the party," I said.

Now that I've been writing awhile, I feel better. But I'm not sure I believe Blackie about Farouk. She just can't come out and admit that she doesn't know. Not a damn thing I can do about it anyway.

Still, I kinda miss seeing his feet sticking out that doorway.

Now I wonder why I ever let Blackie get the best of me that first year. Granted, I never could scope her; but I can scope everyone else. I should have seen what she did to people when she was at her worst. Or even her best.

I wasn't impressed with her the first time I met her. Didn't even like her. Maybe because of Knossos. I was hanging around with him every chance I got, and his shadow eclipsed everyone else.

He and I were going to the pits regularly. He never bought new clothes to replace those rags of his, though. I thought he was sharing his money with other Skids, because they always wanted to talk to him about something or other. Whenever Knossos speaks, everyone listens.

Blackie was just some girl who had free food.

Drugs, too, because by then my loki habit was firmly established. She invited me to stay, and I didn't see any reason why not.

"Those shades are so cool," she told me. "I just wanna dress you up so bad! *Shade*. I mean—just *Shade!*"

Like I said before, Blackie comes on like a ton of bricks at first.

Jake, who was new with her then and who wanted everyone to know she was off limits, hated me at first sight. "I seen you before," he said. "Hanging out with pussy-for-sale at the Baby School."

I was wearing rag-wraps and cropping my hair with a knife in those days, so that was a pretty serious accusation. Everyone was waiting for my answer.

"Yeah," I said. "They asked me to tell you they're saving your bed for you. They know you're gonna want to use it again soon."

He gave me The Look and I gave it right back. I could tell already that Jake is as selfish about fighting as he is about everything else.

Blackie would have squeezed my ass then, but I wouldn't let her. I wanted it clear that I planned to do absolutely nothing in exchange for her food and stuff. And at first I believed that was true.

Knossos noticed the change in me. Once when we were walking alone, he said, "Shade. Why don't you respect yourself?"

I turned red. In fact, I almost cried. "What do you mean?"

"I always say what I mean. It reduces confusion."

Well, that left it up to me. Talking about myself was not something I was eager to do in those days.

"It's just this girl I'm living with right now. She really makes me mad."

"Are you going to ask her to leave?"

"It's her house."

I guess I thought he would say "Oh, I see" or "Of course, that's different." Instead, he said something in a voice so cold and remote it made me feel like we were walking on a glacier.

"So you've traded your self-respect for shelter."

I could hardly believe what I was hearing. I had to look at him to make sure it was really him speaking.

"I've seen too many good soldiers do what you're doing. It saddens me."

"Who are you talking about?" I said. "Me? I'm not like that! I take care of myself!"

He turned his head and looked down at me. Made me feel like shriveling up and crawling away.

"I could leave any time!" I said.

"To have a choice and disregard it is a coward's tactic."

"What's so great about self-respect anyway?" I yelled. "What the hell good does it do on a planet where all you're worth is what people are willing to pay for your ass?"

"Self-respect is the only thing that keeps the soul alive," said Knossos. "Without it there is only room for corruption and despair. When you see people cheating and stealing from each other, Shade—when you see them doing monstrous things to children—do you think you're different from them?"

"Yes!"

"Then don't merely *think*. *Be*."

We stopped and watched some tinkers tearing

down one of the old buildings in Midtown. They
were going to replace it with one of the new
pre-fabs. The new building would look nice for a
while, but it wouldn't last even half as long as
the old one.

"I have so little I can teach the young," Knossos
said. "I have lived with old soldiers too long. But
one thing I do know. Love yourself, Shade. Don't
accept anything less."

I still couldn't see exactly how that applied to
Blackie. Not until I left her. Then I could see
how she had jerked me around and sapped my
energy. Without her around, my scoping ability
was sharper than my best knife.

I know Blackie a lot better now, so she can't
manipulate me like she did before. Once I'm
sure Shade the Deadtowner has been out of sight
and out of mind long enough, I'll leave Blackie to
her destiny. Maybe she'll surprise me and climb
out of her pit.

But I bet she ends up just like her mother,
instead.

Anyway, I've come to a decision. I haven't tried
to follow Snag or Mira since the day by the river.
If Knossos paid off his ship, he may be planning
to leave Z'taruh. I know he plans to pay me the
money he owes me. An elephant never forgets.
But that could be ten years from now.

I've got to find him and convince him to take
me with him. Because I have a feeling that if I
don't get off this planet soon, I never will.

Jake and Blackie are screaming. Farouk's feet
are still absent from the doorway. I found Knossos
today.

*   *   *

I meant to write about what happened with Knossos. I should just start at the beginning and tell how I followed Snag again. But all I can think about right now is what Knossos said to me the last time we went to the pits together.

We had gone for a drink afterward. My head was full of schemes, mostly involving Knossos and other worlds. If I could talk him into betting more of our winnings, I could buy some I.D. papers. After that we could go anywhere.

"You ever think about leaving Z'taruh?" I asked him. He looked at me as if I had just pulled him back from another galaxy. Now that I think of it, Knossos had looked that way for the past year. It made my throat feel a little tight.

"What would you do with your life if you were not here?" he asked me.

"I don't know. Go to college?"

"I don't think so."

"Okay. I'd hit every pit fight and poker game in the galaxy and rake in the dough."

"Is that all?"

The question made me uncomfortable. "Well, I'd like to Space Out I guess. Might be interesting to go with one of the exploration missions, or—" I broke off, knowing that wasn't right. I never paid any more attention to science than I had to, and those probe missions can go on for months without anything happening.

"Space," Knossos said. "Is that why you left home?"

I wondered what he was getting at. Knossos never talks just to hear his own voice.

"Yes," I said, "and no. I needed to make my own way."

"From what I have learned of humans, you were young to be striking out on your own."

"My mother went to Europe and never came back," I blurted. "And I barely remember my father. Why would I want to stay on that crummy planet? The good money's out here."

He nodded without a trace of sympathy or moral outrage. That was a relief.

"I left home at a very young age too," he said. "I became a soldier. I was a younger son, and the military was my only chance to forge a dynasty of my own."

And now he was on a filthy backwater planet. I took a couple of healthy pulls on my drink before I looked at him again.

"If I gave you my word," I said. "I would mean it."

He gazed at me for a long time, but I knew he understood me. "I believe you," he said.

I guess believing me wasn't enough.

The morning I followed Snag, Blackie and Jake had the biggest fight I've ever seen. They had both been eating stims and staying up all night, Blackie babbling about how sleep is just a waste of time and just think of all the things you could get done if you could stay awake! So at all hours I was hearing the two of them bouncing off the walls, until they finally turned on each each like a couple of pit-rats. That fight must have lasted about twenty-four hours, because they were still doing it when I came back.

Maybe I'll get used to it.

I had a hunch about where Snag could be found again. So I went to Medusa's for the morning rat-fights, disguising myself as usual, and hung out in the crowd. Sure enough, he was there by late morning, all bright-eyed about watching his favorite kind of meal hop around and bleed. He didn't bet any money. Just mumbled to himself.

But maybe those rats are too big and mean for even Snag's appetite, because after a while he lost interest and walked off. I followed, scoping like mad. No way was he gonna catch me this time.

He stopped at the S.A., but came right out again. I didn't even have a chance to poke my head in to see who he was talking to. Then he hopped a transport and went all the way out to the pits. But it was the animal show he really seemed to be interested in, because he rolled right across the field and in through the front gate.

I was glad for the thick crowd in there. I could get much closer to him without being seen. I could even hear his reply when some Skid yelled, "Hey Snag! Why don't you go to see the Man Who Eats Live Lizards show!"

He yelled back a curse in Q'rin that I assume is supposed to be extra nasty when said by one Allied Ragnir vet to another. The Skid turned white, but Snag was already out of range.

He went past the big cats and the marine section, and finally stopped in front of the scorpion woman. She was making her pets do tricks by undulating certain parts of her body, so the crowd was enthralled. After a while that young elephant man walked up and stood next to Snag. They watched for a few minutes and then left together.

None of the Q'rin-dogs paid any attention to them as they walked back across the field. I guess they only worry about Aesopians getting together.

When they hopped a transport, I had a pretty good idea where they were heading. Sure enough, they rode to the end of the line, out where the ruins and warehouses litter the edge of town. I just hoped they weren't headed out for the swamps again. I didn't want to meet any rats face-to-knee.

I was getting close. I could feel it. I was already wondering what Blackie would think when I didn't come back. Would she say I had told her I was moving out, like Farouk?

I was glad when they went into a warehouse instead of heading out into the wilderness. I knew I couldn't go in through the same door they did. Didn't want any Ragnir vets bashing my head in before I could tell them who I was. The warehouses in that district looked to be from the same construction period as the Baby School, and that meant sub-levels. I poked around in the building next door until I found a bolt-hole.

The sub-level rooms had water in them. Big surprise.

It was spooky looking down into that wet darkness. There was about a three-foot gap between the water and the ceiling, at least at that point. I was sure slimy things were swimming around down there. But I guess I sort of looked at it like this was some heroic trial I had to perform in order to reach my goal. I was locked into this stupid dreamy notion, determined to do things the hard way. I should have turned right around and marched up to the front door. The end result would have been the same. But I was afraid to be so direct. I couldn't face that then, but I know it now.

Into the warm, smelly water, with no light after the first few feet. I had ditched Blackie's wig and removed my shades—I wished I had left the skirt behind, too. I moved in the direction of Knossos's warehouse, ignoring the gunk and slime my hands encountered. Or trying to, anyway. It shouldn't have been more than a hundred feet or so, but I had to feel all over with my hands, so it took forever.

Pretty soon I felt the current. It gave me an uneasy feeling, like I was being stroked by some dark, silky creature. I could hear the sound of water splashing, probably emptying into a lower level. I felt something furry and fat drift past my legs. My whole body shook with disgust.

I found a grating with my hands. I hoped it belonged to a Shade-sized air shaft, like the ones at the Baby School. I had pounded at it for what felt like forever when it finally came loose.

There was plenty of room in the shaft, and it was dry. I was so relieved to be out of the water, I couldn't move for a while. But pretty soon the air blowing across my face revived me and I got going again.

I looked for another grating in the ceiling of the vent. I didn't have far to go. Light poured in about twenty feet around the next corner, and voices too. Aesopian voices. I thought I heard Knossos. My heart pounded against my ribs like a fist.

I pushed the vent out and stood up. I was right in the middle of the room, where everyone could see me, looking about three feet tall with my legs still in the shaft.

Knossos was there. Snag and the young elephant man jumped about a foot. I got a quick look at a room full of Aesopians, Skids, and even a few Q'rin, before Knossos's eyes pinned me to the floor like a bug.

I said, "Hi. I need to talk to you about something."

I knew I had made a mistake even before I opened my mouth, because of the look on Knossos's face. It was the first time I had ever seen that kind of anger directed at *me*. I felt like I was about to fly apart into a million pieces, but I just stuck my chin out and stood there like a fool.

"If I had wanted to talk to you," Knossos said in a quiet, scary kind of voice, "I would have sent for you."

My face felt very hot all of a sudden, and some of the men standing around started to chuckle. I wanted to kill them.

"You never said I had to wait to be asked," I said.

"Don't use that tone with me."

"Don't talk to me like a kid!" I screamed, losing my cool completely. I was instantly sorry for it. I *was* a damned kid. I had just proved it. "I just—I just—"

"You just need to mind your own business," Knossos said. "You just need to behave like a young woman instead of a spoiled child—"

Snag hissed, interrupting him. "Sneaky Shade! I never heard you this time. My fault for forgetting your nose too big for your brain."

The men laughed again. I forgot everything I had planned to say about how I wanted to be included and what an asset I could be. I couldn't think of anything to say at all.

"If I catch you following me again," Snag continued, "I lash your behind until you got nothing to sit down on!"

"Yeah," I croaked. "Right."

"Go home now," Knossos said. "You have forgotten everything I tried to tell you. I'm disappointed."

It was just as well that a lion man and a bear man took hold of my arms at that point and dragged me out of there, because I wouldn't have been able to move on my own. The last thing I remember as they hauled me out the door is Snag shaking his head and muttering "Nosy girl, nosy girl."

They dragged me all the way to the transport line. "You are lucky Lord Knossos doesn't put you in chains," the lion man told me. "I hope his trust in you is justified."

His trust in *me*.

But I was actually quite happy to be dragged along in those big furry hands, even with their claws tickling my armpits. Because I still couldn't walk right. I had forgotten how to move. They waited with me for the transport, paid the driver, and watched the transport drive away. As I looked out the window at them I finally recognized them; Rorra and Ousa, the wrestlers. Rorra actually started to wave at me, until Ousa stuck an elbow in his gut.

I rode that transport for most of the day. I couldn't even think. My skirt dried and assumed a distorted shape. I was so voided I forgot I wasn't wearing my shades or my wig.

A pair of elegant shoes moved into my line of sight as someone sat down in the seat across from mine. My eyes traveled up the thin legs, up an equally thin torso, to a porcelain face. The Lyrri gazed at me soulfully, as if I were a painting.

"What beautiful eyes you have."

I realized she was a woman when she said that. Her voice. That's the only way you can tell a male and a female Lyrri apart, unless you look between their legs. Or unless you scope, which I wasn't doing. I was sitting there stinking and airing an empty mind. Maybe that's why she didn't proposition me. She must have thought I was a mobile art display.

I didn't even have the sense to be glad it wasn't Chaz sitting across from me.

I'm glad I thought of that, because now I remember what's really important. Even if everything else is shit, I don't want to die. I still like to eat and sleep and smoke loki. If nothing else looks good, I'll concentrate on those things.

No one concentrates better than me.

Jake is gone for good. He wrecked the place before he left. He came up to my room and stood in the doorway, looking like a ghost.

"Guess it's just you and her now," he said.

I was sitting up, having been awake through the whole mess. I thought he had come up to kick my ass, but he just slumped there like an old man. One of his eyes was swollen shut.

"She trampled you pretty good," I said. "You two would have put on a good show at the pits."

"Who would you have bet on?"

"No contest," I said. "You know that."

He did now. It's funny to talk about a Dead-towner becoming disillusioned, but that was the situation. He came farther into the room and stood looking into Farouk's door. I felt he was on the verge of telling me something, or maybe he already had and I had missed it.

"Are you leaving?" I asked.

"Yeah. So the two of you can get cozy now. Nothing to stop you."

"I'd rather have you between Blackie and me any day. Don't know how much longer I'll be able to stand it myself."

When he sighed, it was like his crutch had been knocked out from under him. His knuckles almost touched the floor.

"Okay," he said. "I know." He pulled out a stick of loki and lit it. After a long pull he seemed to feel a little better. He handed it to me and looked me in the eye while I took my turn. I wouldn't have scoped him then for anything. I didn't want to know.

After he left, I looked in on Blackie. She was sound asleep. I was relieved. I found a whole shitload of loki and smoked a few more sticks.

The place is full of drugs and food. Also more booze than I've ever seen here. Blackie must have scored big again. That's why she and Jake were celebrating with the stims. Now she'll probably sleep for a couple of days. That's what she always does.

I've got to get out of here. For a few hours, at least. I've been looking at that card Mr. Field gave me. I wonder what he would do if I just showed up at his office. If he throws me out, I don't really care. I've been thrown out by the best.

"Do you always dress like that?" Mr. Field said.

"I have no taste," I said.

"And no money."

"More than you think. I do well at the pits."

Don't know why I told him that. He was a nice

man, and it bothered him. I guess I wanted to be honest right at the beginning so I wouldn't have to keep making dumb stuff up. His office was a no-nonsense, no-fills kinda place, and he was wearing work clothes. I was sitting in the heart of tinker territory, and all my cards were on the table.

"I play killer poker, too," I said.

"If you want to get a game together you'll have to wait 'til Wednesday," he said. "That's our regular day."

"When's Wednesday?"

He turned his back on me and looked out a big plexi-window that gave him an overview of Deadtown. Somehow, that view made me respect him more, silly as that may sound.

"Are you looking for a job?" he asked.

"I don't know."

"I see a lot of desperate kids in here. If they're sixteen or older I give them what work I can. If they're younger, I steer them toward the Salvation Army or the shelter in Midtown."

I settled deeper into the big, comfortable chair he had for visitors. "You do more than most," I said.

"I turn my back on things I could never have ignored before. It's this planet. It turns your eyes to stone. So, do you want a job?"

"How do you know I need one?"

He turned away from his window and sat down at his desk. "You were with Blackie. I know she lives in Deadtown."

"What I really want is a place to go during the day," I said. "Something to do besides watch Blackie sleep it off—or worse, deal with Blackie wide awake."

"What I really need is a receptionist," he said. "Someone tough, perceptive, and smart. The last guy quit when an Aesopian threw him out the window. He was a bigot, and probably brought it on himself. Good receptionist, though."

I laughed, even though the image brought back painful memories. "I've got to tell you something," I said. "I hate tinkers."

He didn't say anything to that, so I went on.

"The job you're describing is easy," I said, "but I'll have to accept it on a trial basis."

"I'm the one who's supposed to say that."

"It's the same thing."

"Can you start now?"

I did. Worked for six hours answering the com, scribbling notes, talking to visitors, and working on Mr. Field's appointment schedule. I had all the supervisors pegged after the first hour or so; they were all right. Mr. Field is a pretty good judge of character. Except for mine, of course.

He didn't ask me my address, but he asked me to call in if I couldn't make it. And I signed a bunch of papers that gave him permission to pay me in cash and take out the standard taxes.

"Lots of workers prefer it that way," he said.

I did too.

When I got back to Blackie's, she was still asleep. I made supper and listened to music, pretending I was in my own place.

If I could feel, I might even enjoy the situation. The most I can do now is appreciate it.

I worked for Mr. Field for an entire work day. Blackie is still asleep. I'm taking regular showers now.

*　　*　　*

Poker day finally rolled around. Mr. Field dragged a bunch of chairs into his office, and we all sat around his desk. I was sitting with a bunch of tinkers and an accountant. She didn't say much, and seemed very serious about the game, like she thought she could manipulate the cards the same way she manipulates numbers. She was a good player.

I tried not to win more than half the hands. Mr. Field, the accountant (Jesse something), and I went home with the money. They all sort of like me, probably because Mr. Field does.

When I got home, Blackie was awake. She was making tons of black coffee and squinting at everything. "Jake said he was moving out," she said.

"Mmm. Want something to eat?"

"No. Just gonna pour some whiskey in this coffee."

This was Blackie's Dr. Jekyll I was talking to, a person too burned out and tired to be crazy. It's during times like these that she can be reasoned with, if at all. I hope it lasts a few days, because even the static has died down. When I scope her, all I get is ashes.

The two of us slumped down in her living room, me unwinding and her trying to get started. Now that she was awake, I became more aware of the scars of her battle with Jake, which marked everything in the room but her. And me. I don't know if she sees them or not.

"Wanna go out with me tomorrow?" she asked.

"Maybe tomorrow night. Got something to do during the day."

"Fine."

Yeah, I like it when she's like this.

*　　*　　*

So I guess I'll give this job thing a chance. It keeps me busy. I see all kinds of people; even the Q'rin Lords do some business with Mr. Field.

I wonder if that's how Donokh found out I was working there.

That still doesn't explain how he found me and Blackie behind Club Draggit. He must have been watching for awhile.

Despite the fact that I have spending money now, I still would rather sit behind a club than inside it. Especially Draggit's, which will break your skull with the volume if you get too close. Blackie brought her drinks and I brought my loki, and we made a sort of picnic in the alley. She was mellow. I guess I was more relaxed than usual too, really enjoying my leisure time.

We heard the sound of boots on gravel, and Donokh walked up. He waited long enough to see if I recognized him, then spoke to Blackie.

"Leave us."

Blackie looked hurt.

"Don't move," I told her.

"Go," he said, and she practically ran.

He sat down in her place and gave me a long look. I stared at my feet.

"I heard a rumor that you had died at the Baby School," he said. "But later I saw you at the pits with the Special One. Though you didn't want to see me."

"Surprised?"

"I had nothing to do with the raid at the Baby School," he said.

"Okay, but if you had gotten the order—"

"I don't do that kind of work. I'm not a mercenary. I'm a soldier—the kind who only takes orders from *superiors*—and no soldier took part in that raid."

For some reason I was beginning to feel like a bigot. I scoped him. He meant what he was saying.

"So how come you're looking for me?" I asked.

"I want to know about Knossos," he lied. Or at least half-lied. But I took the question seriously.

"I don't have anything to do with him anymore," I said, as I pulled out another stick of loki.

"Nothing?"

"Not a damn thing."

"You sound disappointed."

I had to take several long pulls on the stick to keep my throat and nasal passages open. They seemed to want to close down and get all wet. I could feel Donokh leaning closer, and then his hand was on my face, making me look at him.

"You don't know Knossos," I said. "He was like my father or my teacher. When we bet together, we couldn't lose. Now he doesn't know me."

"If he would have you, would you follow him?"

"He won't, so there's no point in talking about it."

I don't know how it got there, but his arm was around me. His rocky face was shadowed.

"Do you know what the penalty is if you are caught conspiring with an Aesopian to commit civil disobedience?"

"That could cover a lot," I said.

"To us it means only one thing. It means the defeated are conspiring to overthrow the victors. The penalty is slow dismemberment."

I didn't think he wanted to do that to me. But I didn't want to push him, either.

"Are you going to haul me in?"

His hand tightened on my hip. "I hear you're working for the tinker Field, now. You're not a Deadtowner anymore. I have no right to harrass an honest citizen without good cause."

"You mean a human citizen."

He grinned. Very sharp teeth.

"We are all careful these days; you humans because you don't want history to blame you, and we Q'rin because we don't want to waste time and energy in street brawls."

"You don't want the house of cards to come down," I said.

"What?"

"The house of cards. You lean cards together and carefully build a house. It takes a long time, and one puff will knock it down. So you don't want anyone else to get near it. Z'taruh is like that. Everyone agrees to stay away from everyone else's house in order to protect their own."

I barely got that last part out before he kissed me. I was surprised, but only because I thought Q'rin went in more for love bites. His lips were hard, but they set off all kinds of hot little fires in my body. I bet it was the best kiss I've ever had.

I think we were there for a long time. I'm not sure. Finally he leaned back to look at me. He seemed cooler than I was. He slipped off my shades, which were steamed up anyway.

"You've put on some weight," he said. "It's very becoming."

"I get regular meals."

"And this is not your real hair," he said, touching the long, red stuff on my head. "This is what fooled me before."

That was good to know.

"Stay away from Knossos," he said. "I can't protect you if you're caught with him."

"No problem."

He slipped something out of his pocket and pushed it into my hand. It was a thin, metal triangle with Q'rin symbols on it. "If you want me, come to Red Station. Two stops on the transport from the pits. This card will get you in."

He stood up and tossed my shades to me. "Too bad you're not a Deadtowner anymore. I wouldn't have to wait for you to come to me. I could just knock you out and drag you in."

I think he was just flirting with me, Q'rin style. I gave him a flirty smile of my own and put my shades back on.

"I'll see you around," he said, and went away, those long legs of his eating up the ground.

When he was gone, I thought about the kiss. My glasses were still steamy. But I'm not sure I could handle a Q'rin penis. Never seen one, but I've heard about 'em. I might not be able to walk for weeks.

Maybe it's a good thing Knossos will never see this notebook after all.

I found Blackie at the bar. "I can't believe he went after you like that!" she said. "What did he want?"

"Nothing."

"Come on, Shade! Was it—like, something about the pits?"

"It was personal."

That shut her up. I peeked at her after a few moments and saw the madonna smile fixed tightly into place. Her bright gaze was darting back and forth around the room. This was strange. Why

would she care if I had a thing with Donokh?
She couldn't have been scandalized. Not this girl.

The band started blasting away again, so it
was impossible to talk or—as far as I was concerned
—think anymore. I put up with it for an hour for
Blackie's sake. Then I got up and walked out.

I was surprised when Blackie followed. "You
don't have to leave because of me," I said.

"You're my friend," she said curtly.

"Well, shit, what does that have to do with
it?"

She slugged me in the arm. "Shade, don't be
such an asshole, okay? Just—don't."

I sighed, saying farewell to Dr. Jekyll.

"I'm going to talk to Jake about that Q'rin-
dog," she announced.

"I didn't know you and he were still talking."

"Of course we are! We're just—like—friends
now. We get along better that way."

"When did you decide that?"

"Just before he moved out."

She had already forgotten that I had witnessed
that last fight.

"Don't bother," I said. "It's none of Jake's
business."

I saw her fist coming from the corner of my
eye, so I managed to duck and just miss it.

"You bitch!" Blackie was shrieking. "You stuck
up, know-it-all-bitch! You think you can do anything! You think you're so tough and skinny and
everyone wants your cunt! *You make me sick!*"

She took a few more swings at me, but I just
stepped out of the way. Her face turned white,
and her eyes got huge.

"You're just like everyone else, Shade," she
panted. "You're not a Deadtowner anymore. So

don't go acting like you're better than me just because I never got to wear rag-wraps and plasti-fix—"

She choked and started to cry. I got the feeling she wanted me to hug her, but that was the last thing in the world I wanted to do.

"You could wear rag-wraps if you wanted to," I said.

"They wouldn't let me," she sobbed.

"Who? Your parents?"

She slapped at me, even though she knew I was out of range. "Deadtowners!" she said. "Deadtowners! You would laugh at me. I hate it when people make fun of me!'"

"So what? Do it anyway."

She was drying her face now, but she still looked mad. "I care too much what people think."

"You sure do," I said. Though I noticed she didn't pay any attention to the people who stared at us as they walked past us.

"I can do anything I set my mind to," she said.

"Huh?" I wondered if I had missed something.

"I don't wear rag-wraps because—like—I just like shopping too much. I like clothes, you know? And I'm good at putting them together." She gave me a smug little smile.

"So what are we arguing about?"

"I designed these—like—Deadtowner clothes. Only they're for rich kids and government brats. You know, posers." She giggled, then gave me a forlorn look.

"Don't hate me, Shade."

"I don't." That would take too much energy.

"It's just, you always act like you don't give a damn."

"Actually," I said, "I don't. I've eaten garbage

for two years now, Blackie. What do you want from me?"

"I know I'll never be as cool as you," she said. "But that doesn't mean you have to treat me like shit."

I couldn't believe it. She was trying to get me to apologize. After screaming at me and swinging at me, she felt she deserved one. I wasn't about to do it. It was time to get tough.

I pulled out a stick of loki. "I've been thinking about moving out," I said, looking at my feet.

"You don't have to do that," she whimpered.

"No, really." I lit the stick and sucked on it. "It would probably be for the best."

"Well—like—where would you go?"

"That's not the issue. I don't like being slugged. You tried to kick my ass tonight. I don't like that."

"You deserved it!" she hissed. Then she seemed to think better of it. "You know I can't hit you if you don't want me to."

"I never want to be hit."

"Well, of course not—"

"Okay," I said. "Then let's call a truce. No hitting, and we stay out of each other's private lives."

It took her some time to agree to that, but at least we both knew there wasn't going to be any apology from me.

I'm not really ready to move out of Blackie's place. I'm not sure I'm going to keep working for Mr. Field, and even if I wanted to pay for my own place, all I could afford would be one of those tiny box houses the government workers live in. No way. But Blackie would do anything to keep me from leaving now. She's terrified of being alone.

We walked home instead of taking a transport. I think we both needed to work the hostility out of our systems. As we walked through the public square near the fast-food stalls, we ran into five Lyrri-dogs who were obviously cruising. Seeing them made my guts turn to ice, even though Chaz wasn't with them. I was sick as I waited for Blackie to blow it by smiling at them or by making eye contact, but she didn't. What a relief!

I'll bet Chaz has forgotten all about me by now. He probably was only after me because he figured no one would notice if I disappeared. Anyway, I haven't seen him.

But I have to admit, I haven't been looking.

For days and days now, the Q'rin have been marching in and out of Mr. Field's office, and Mr. Field has been looking more and more worried. Today one of the Lords himself came down for a visit. Stood there looking at a spot over my head while his second spoke to me. He and his second went into Field's office, leaving four dogs in the outer office to stare at me. I could have scoped them, but I didn't really want to know what they thought of me.

The Lord came out again, and as he passed my desk he glanced down at me. I scoped a strange combination of nobility and jaded curiosity. Once he was gone, Field called me into his office.

He was sitting in his chair and staring out at Deadtown. I sat down and waited, feeling waves of worry flowing out of him.

"Well," he said, "I've just been offered the deal of a lifetime."

When he didn't say anything more, I said, "You don't sound too happy about it."

"I'm not sure whether to be happy or not. I've done business with Lord Oshrii before—he always sticks right to the letter of an agreement, but he bargains like a barracuda—anyway, he deals with me exclusively now. He likes my work."

He glanced at me, looking completely dazed. He poured a cup of coffee from the hotkeeper on his desk and offered it to me. His hand was steady.

"Did you know the biggest struggle that's going on in Capital right now is over Deadtown? Nobody owns most of the property, because nobody wants to be responsible for it. But if you're willing to knock down a building and build something in its place, it's yours. Hell of a lot of work, even with the best equipment. If you want to build something that will last, it takes more money than most people are willing to spend."

He laughed.

"Those cheap bastards on the Hill are going to be furious. Well. The Q'rin Lords want to take down one-third of Deadtown and build a fortress there. Offices, barracks—stuff like that. Why do you think they want to do it?"

An uneasy feeling was creeping up my spine. "Because they're tired of living in a house of cards," I said.

He frowned. "Yeah. But what's the point? Z'taruh isn't a strategic planet—at least, as far as I know. This is a great place to make money if you're a developer or the owner of a casino."

Or a drug lord or a Baby peddler.

"The Q'rin were here before anyone else," I said. "The Aesopians, too. That's what I heard. After the war, they didn't care who else came here."

"It's funny," he said. "I think they still don't care."

The two of us stared out the window at those ugly buildings. They were the first of the pre-fab structures humans built when we arrived here. They're decaying, but they make the new pre-fab stuff look like cardboard.

"They want to use the best materials," Field said. "Adamantium, marble, transparent aluminum, some stuff they even want to bring from their home planet, uh—Zorin. Where do you suppose they'll get the money?"

"Probably from conquered planets."

"Yeah," he sighed. "I wonder if there's any other kind of money."

"Not on this planet."

"Oshrii has offered me enough money to buy five more companies like this one. Let me tell you Shade—that, combined with the fact that we'll be using decent materials for a change, is very tempting. I would be able to offer my employees steady work for the next ten years. With excellent pay."

Too bad most of it will end up in the casinos.

"Sounds like a good deal to me," I said.

"Could be. Or it could put me right in the middle of a war."

"Maybe. But once people see what kind of wages you're offering, and the casino owners start getting some of the kickback, I'll bet you become a popular guy. Besides, the Q'rin-dogs will protect you."

"Oh, God." He rubbed his face like he was trying to take it off. "Whether I say yes or no, things are going to get ugly."

"So what happens if you say no? Someone else

takes the job, and you lose all that money, and your best employees, plus some of your biggest clients."

"Tell me about it," he said, then smiled. "By the way, we're invited to the pit fights with Oshrii this Saturday. Fanciest seats in the house."

"You and me?!"

"Yeah. Angie wouldn't go if her life depended on it, and I know you like the fights."

Angie is Mrs. Field. I guess she's okay, but she's not good enough for him. Come to think of it, neither am I.

"You say Oshrii is going to sit with us?"

"Supposed to."

"You think we could arrange for me to sit next to him?"

His eyebrows went up. "I don't know. Why?"

"Well, uh, you know I'm good at poker, right?"

"Right . . ."

"And you know that I win at poker because I watch everyone's faces and decide what they're doing, right?"

"I don't know. If you say so."

"Well, it's sort of the same thing."

He stared at me for a long moment, and I was glad, once again, to have the shades in place. Telling him all that was kind of showing off, but I thought maybe I could make some money for him and for myself.

"Remind me to give you a raise," he said.

That's okay by me.

So when they demolish those buildings in Deadtown, they'll implode them. They'll fall in on themselves and raise clouds of dust that will float around for days, maybe months. For a little while, Deadtown will be an even better place for

Deadtowners to hang out. Then the dust will clear, and the Q'rin fortress will be there—and where will the Deadtowners go? Maybe the boundaries will change again, flow into another decaying part of town.

Or maybe the Q'rin will hunt all the Deadtowners down. Don't know if I should tell Mr. Field about that or not. It would just make him more miserable.

When the old buildings are demolished, they'll haul the debris away and dump it in the swamps at the edge of town. No one cares. Maybe it just seems natural for Capital to be a zit on the face of Z'taruh, all crusty on the outside and infected on the inside. Everyone knows it. But just as long as everyone can keep buying pussy, loki, gambling thrills, and submarine sandwiches, it's all right.

I wonder how much of a raise I'm going to get.

I got up this morning, long before Blackie could stagger out of bed, and hopped a transport for Mr. Field's office. He was waiting for me there. He looked a little depressed, like there were probably a hundred things he would rather be doing. I toned down my excitement for his benefit.

Pretty soon a Q'rin transport came along and picked us up. Our two escorts and the driver treated us politely, if stiffly, and Mr. Field relaxed a little.

"They don't serve booze at the pits," I told him. "But I'll bet Oshrii has his own private flask."

"This early in the morning? I'm not that much of a drinker, Shade. And I'm not that squeamish."

"Just telling you."

He didn't seem to take the idea seriously, so I figured he was okay. Our escorts watched us out of the corners of their eyes, trying to take our measure. I think we came off pretty well.

When we arrived at the pits, we went around to an entrance I'd never seen before. We passed through a maze of tunnels that actually took us past some of the workout rooms. Hardly anyone except the pit fighters and other personnel ever see that place. Even Mr. Field seemed interested by the sights. We passed on up to the privileged seating, boxes the powerful families have held forever. Oshrii sat waiting for us, his back as straight as a rod.

"Good morning, Field," he said. "I see you brought your receptionist."

"Yes," Field said. "This is Shade."

"You've been to the pits before," Oshrii said to me. I wondered if he knew exactly how many times and with whom. He acted like he did.

"Yes," I said. "Are you a bettor or a watcher?"

"A bettor."

"Then maybe you won't mind if I sit next to you, so we can discuss the fighters."

"Please do," he said.

Mr. Field and I exchanged brief looks as we sat down. He looked pleased that I had handled the situation well. Maybe he didn't know that there had been a good chance that Oshrii would refuse to sit with me, seeing as how I'm the employee of an employee. We were lucky.

Still, I'd rather sit with the ordinary crowd. Oshrii's box was crowded with escorts; and though they all looked unruffled, I scoped a dangerous undercurrent. Only Oshrii and Field were completely relaxed—Field because he couldn't read the tension, and Oshrii because he was even more aware of what was going on around him than I was.

That became very evident when the fights started.

Two Aesopian wrestlers started the day. This time they were both bear men. They looked exactly alike. When I scoped them, I could see one of them was an amateur and the other was a female. The amateur was talented, but still—

"Gee," I said to Oshrii, "they look exactly alike."

"They do," he said, "but they don't move alike. Winna is a seasoned professional. She has been known to beat Rorra, the best wrestler on Z'taruh."

He saw them very clearly. He probably would make as good a betting partner as Knossos. But it felt weird to scope through someone who has been certain of his own superiority from the day he could walk. The fact that he's such a keen observer only makes it more oppressive. If you're not used to being wrong, it's hard to recognise what few mistakes you do make.

Anyway, I bet our money on Winna. The other guy was an amateur, and as they stood there looking at each other I could see he was a little intimidated by her. As soon as they got the start signal, she went barrelling into him like a freight train, and the two of them hit the ground hard enough to make it shake. My eardrums even popped. Winna was on top, and though he did manage to flip her off before she could pin him, he was definitely shaken. Most wrestlers are much more refined and aloof in their style, and I had the distinct impression that she had actually *embarrassed* him!

She threw him four more times in short order,

popping my ears twice more and raising a cloud of dust. The poor guy found it a little harder to get up each time, but he kept trying, and even managed to almost pin her near the end. But she foiled him by licking his ear. He jumped to his feet, holding his ear as if it had been burned, and I'm sure he was blushing under all that fur. Winna was immediately up and on him. He realized what she was doing too late, and couldn't stop her. She had him pinned in a moment.

Oshrii's men grumbled a little at the ploy Winna had used, but Oshrii laughed. "There's nothing in the rules about licking your opponent's ear," he said. "Besides, we won."

That was how I saw it, too.

"You want me to bet some more?" I asked Mr. Field.

"Sure," he said. He was smiling. I think he enjoyed the wrestling more than he thought he would.

The next two bouts were wrestlers too, because today was challenge match day instead of the variety schedule. I continued to scope through Oshrii, and win for Field and myself.

I was happy when the Lectrowhippers came out. Timmy and another hot fighter, Oscar X. Poor Field went a little pale. I didn't ask him if he wanted to bet on this one. I didn't scope through Oshrii either, because I could see Timmy was the obvious winner. Oscar X is human; and though he's good enough to challenge Timmy and live, today she still had to be the one who would make the most points.

And she did. He put up a good fight, though, waiting for her to make the first hit. He couldn't have done that if he hadn't been an expert at controlling the whip, which was lashing over his head like static before he got to use it. Timmy gave him a nasty burn on his side as he moved away from her cut like the prime athlete he was. He struck at her four times as he moved, using the charge up a little at a time, and leaving him with almost none at the end. That would force Timmy to make the first move again, which actually put her at a disadvantage. By the time she did that, he'd have enough to defend himself with again.

But Timmy didn't wait to build up a big charge. She just kept hitting him with low to medium ones. She knew she was faster and more agile than him; so all she had to do was keep scoring points, cutting him as delicately as a surgeon. He hit back, I'll give him that, and by the time the ref ended the game, she actually looked winded. He looked like hell, but he was still alive and walking.

Since I was the only one who had bet on that bout, I was the only one who won. Mr. Field was rubbing the bridge of his nose. Oshrii was surveying the crowd, casually.

"You didn't bring the elephant man with you today," he said.

That made me sit up straighter.

Did Donokh tell him? Or did he recognize me himself?

"I haven't seen him in a long time," I said. "Anyway, I only bet with him. Didn't know him that well."

"You seem to be very well on your own."

"*Very well* isn't great. Besides, I needed someone to protect my earnings."

"Any dog could have done that."

"I said *protect*. Not take a huge cut."

He gave me a cold look. "So the elephant man is a nobleman, and incapable of cheating. Is that what you think?"

I knew I had to be perfectly honest now. "Well, he never cheated me. And that was why I bet with him."

I waited for him to tell me about the punishment for conspiracy, or to tell me I was under arrest, but he didn't say anything more about it. Maybe it had just been his way of letting Mr. Field know he had checked out his organization. Field seemed curious about our conversation, but the next lectrowhip match gave him other things to think about.

I didn't try to scope through Oshrii anymore. Made me too nervous. He had been right about my betting judgment. I won all but one of the remaining bets. I could have lost a couple more, but that wouldn't have fooled Oshrii.

We didn't have to go to the windows to collect our winnings. A messenger carried them right to us. I suppose most people would prefer that, but I was ready to say goodbye and go home. I know Field felt even more eager to do that, but it was not to be.

"Stay and share the midday meal with me," Oshrii said.

"Thank you," Mr. Field said, without a trace of hesitation.

Shit.

But we got to go back under the pits and have lunch with some of the fighters, so it wasn't all bad. Oshrii is patron to eight major fighters, including Larissa. I was pleased to see her sitting at the table when we got there. With her were six Q'rin fighters, four men and two women.

I found out Timmy is number eight. "She can't join us today," Oshrii explained as we sat down. "She is with the surgeon now."

I'll bet, after that bout with Oscar X. Couldn't say I was sorry, either.

Mr. Field got to sit with Larissa. She winked at me from across the table, but other than that, she devoted her attention to him. "I hear you're going to work with Oshrii on the big project," she said to him.

"We're talking about it," he said, without missing a beat. He may not be a pit-betting man, but he knows how to keep his cool in business. Larissa didn't bring up the subject again.

I wondered just how much Oshrii has her under his thumb. Larissa is terrific, a fighter's fighter. I think it would be a shame if she just turned into another lackey. She's got guts to back up her talent; and unlike some Deadtowners-turned-pit-fighters I've heard about, she's no bully.

But I didn't get to hear much of what she and Field said to each other, because the two wrestlers I was sitting next to really seemed determined to bother me.

"Have you ever had sex with a Q'rin man?" one asked me. His head was completely shaved, except for one short braid.

"None of your business."

"She hasn't," the other one said, the one with the eyebrows that met in the middle, "or she'd show more respect."

"She wouldn't be sitting down, either," said Mr. Braid, and they both laughed. This was all said in Earth Standard, of course, for my benefit.

"Why don't you give it a try?" Mr. One-Brow put his hand on my thigh. "You won't know what a real man feels like until you do."

I brushed his hand away. "No."

"She's scared," said Mr. Braid. "She must have a very small cunt. She thinks we would tear it wide open."

He watched me to see how I would react to his use of an English dirty word (actually I think it was originally French), but I just nibbled on my bread. I didn't look to Oshrii for help. He knows damn well how the anatomy of a human female differs from that of a Q'rin female. I could tell. He was watching me like they were, to see how vulnerable I was and how far I could be pushed.

I took a sip of mineral water and looked Mr. Braid right in the eye. "I'm not scared," I said. "I just don't want you."

Oddly enough, they accepted that.

I was glad when the lunch was over and Oshrii saw us off.

"I'll see you on Monday," he told Mr. Field. "We'll discuss our business further."

"That's fine," said Mr. Field. "I'll be expecting you."

I knew then that he had decided to accept the contract. Oshrii knew it too. He nodded and turned his back, which was our cue to go away.

"So," Field said as we rode the transport home. "You have a good time?"

We only had a Q'rin driver on the way back, and he was one of the regular transport drivers you'll find in the Q'rin sector, so I decided to be honest.

"I enjoyed the fights and talking to Larissa. Forget the rest of it."

"You seemed pretty cool," he said. "I thought I was the only one who was having a rotten time."

"Better get used to it."

"I know. I think along with your raise I'm going to upgrade your job description."

"Uh oh."

He laughed. "You can handle it. You made the day a whole lot easier for me. By the way, who's this 'Knossos' Oshrii was talking about?"

"An ex-friend. Someone who could have gotten me killed. He's not a problem."

"That's good." He gazed out the window at solid Q'rin architecture and armed dogs. "Because whether the people on the Hill know it or not, the Q'rin are the real bosses on this planet. Once this fortress is built, their rules are going to be the only rules that count."

Could be.

Blackie was wide awake when I got home. Stims and coffee. Breakfast of maniacs. She looked ready to eat me. Asked me where I'd been.

"The rat-fights," I said.

Her madonna smile was edged with sharp teeth. She threw something at me, but I dodged it. "Asshole," she said, trying to make it sound like she was joking. But I knew she got the message.

I took as much of her nonsense as I could before coming upstairs. She's down there now, partying with her usual crowd—except for Jake, who's sticking to his word. When they're done, the walls will have a lot more holes.

I hope she sleeps 'til Tuesday.

I've finally worked out what's wrong with Blackie. She's a Puritan. I know it sounds weird, but it's true. It occurred to me this morning, when she and her stim-head friends were still buzzing around from yesterday's dose. I had to smoke two sticks of loki to immunize myself from the hysteria.

"You assholes made me miss my favorite program," she was saying. "*Sanctify Yourself With Brother Burt!* Goddammit! That's two weeks in a row I've missed it."

There were the sorts of hoots and howls you could expect after a comment like that, but Blackie announced in a calm voice, "Don't laugh. I really like that program. I'm a New Christian."

Someone gave her the razz, but I kept my mouth shut. I hadn't heard her spouting that stuff since back when I had my last really hot affair.

It was with this Deadtowner. He had chocolate skin and dredlocks and a big cynical mouth. He wouldn't tell me his name, because he said he would be leaving soon and he didn't want any attachments. He was saving his money to get his I.D. and go off-planet. I assume he made it, because he disappeared right after one of the freighters came in. I missed his mouth, and the way he never climaxed unless he was sure I had first. He never knew he had gotten me pregnant.

So I asked Blackie if she knew where I could get an abortion, and she said, "Why? You can keep the baby and we can raise it right here, together! It'll be fun."

The thought of it still makes me dizzy.

"No way," I said. "I'm not bringing another baby here for them to fuck and eat and spit out. No way."

She argued with me for an hour about it, until finally she said, "What are you going to tell God after you've killed your baby?"

"I don't know. I suppose I'll ask him why he keeps killing his."

To her credit, she did steer me to an abortionist. But I had to listen to religious talk for weeks afterward. And I suppose it made sense. Blackie feels guilty about almost everything she does. Especially sex, and she does that a lot. But the New Christian thing gives her an out, because now Jezuz can forgive her for every rotten thing she does. And continues to do.

It's a perfect situation. Check and balance.

"I love to listen to Brother Burt," Blackie said this morning. "What's, like, the best thing about him is that he—teaches! Just teaches, you know?"

"What does he teach?" I asked her.

She got mad at that.

"Aren't you listening? Just—stop criticizing me, okay?"

Just as I thought. He doesn't teach anything at all. Those vid-preachers just ramble. They keep their message vague and general so they can hook as many people as possible. People have their own interpretation. Blackie's interpretation is: "I'm bad. Everyone else is bad too." That's the Puritan ethic.

I mean, she's against abortion, right? But she knew where to find an abortionist.

I went upstairs to try to get some more rest. They're still banging around down there. All the stuff Blackie stole from her parents' house is broken by now. She woke me up a little while ago to ask me some weird questions.

"Where have you been lately?"

"None of your business."

"I could understand if you were fucking a Lyrri. They're beautiful. But the Q'rin are ugly!"

"You don't fuck Lyrri. You get fucked up by Lyrri."

"Bullshit, Shade! You haven't even tried it!"

"What time is it?"

"You're just letting that Q'rin do what he wants to you because you're afraid to tell him no."

"Is it morning yet?"

"Those stinking Q'rin are trying to take over the whole planet! The Lyrii want everyone to be happy."

"Huh?"

"How can you stand to have one of those big donkey dicks inside you?"

"You wish you had one."

"I'm serious, Shade."

"I'm so tired I can't even think. What are you bothering me for? You just like the Lyrri because they're prettier than the Q'rin."

She didn't answer that. Her static tightened and recoiled like a snake. That's how I knew I had hit home.

"Sometimes you can be such a shithead," she said, and she left me alone.

I couldn't get back to sleep because I was busy thinking about what's wrong with Blackie. I'm just glad I don't have to work today.

I'd forgotten about that—I mean how work can be a problem that way, when you're tired or just don't feel like it. I'm lucky, I guess, because it's interesting to work for Mr. Field. But sometimes when I'm sitting in that office, laughing and talking with tinkers, I remember that tinker who tossed a sub in the gutter when I was hungry.

Some people are willing to fuck themselves up the butt just to hold a job.

A couple of times I've considered calling in sick to Mr. Field and taking a day off. I'd have to lie to him because I wouldn't want to face him with the truth. But if I lie to him I'll get stuck with guilt for wanting to goof off. Just like Blackie.

Anyway, I've gone that route before. Lied to bosses to get free time. Once you do it, it becomes a habit. Eventually you have to face the fact that your boss knows you've lied.

Whatever I do, I'm not going to lie to Mr. Field.

Like I said, the job is interesting. The alternative is to stay home with Blackie. I don't have any reason to walk the old beat anymore, because Knossos doesn't like me. The Babies are dead, and Chaz the Lyrri is after me. I don't even want to go to the Salvation Army anymore—Snag and Mira know what happened with Knossos. I don't want them pitying me or laughing at me.

But I'm still thinking I don't want to work Monday. It's like the day with Oshrii took the wind out of my sails. What would an extra day off hurt?

Those stim-heads are never going to shut up. If they keep it up much longer, I'll have to smoke another stick to get to sleep. Now that I'm working, I can afford a lot more of that stuff. And other stuff, too. With the raise I could probably afford one of the better box-type houses.

Shit. I'd better think about this.

I just went back for this notebook. Didn't try to take anything else—except the clothes on my back and the wig on my head. I'd throw them away too, or burn them. But I need the disguise.

I brought Stone some food, but I guess he's got bad internal injuries, because he won't eat it. Now he's trying to sleep, blowing little bloody bubbles from his mouth.

I got sick of Blackie and her friends, so I decided to take a walk. Before I could get out the door, Blackie flew at me like a bird of prey.

"Shade wait! You have to try on the clothes I made!"

"How about when I get back?"

"Please? Pleasepleasepleasepleaseplease?"

"Christ. Okay, just for a few minutes."

She hauled me back to her dressing room and practically tore the dress off my body. The wig, too.

"Your Deadtown haircut is growing out," she gloated.

I let it pass, because I didn't give a shit. She pulled a bunch of junk off one of the racks and threw it in a pile. Then she waves this thing in my face.

It was sort of a body suit. Only it was made to look like rag-wraps. It even had torn edges and gaps here and there. It also had these weird glittery threads shot all through it. Silver and gold. Kind of reminded me of something, though I didn't know what yet.

"Put it on!" she demanded.

I couldn't touch it. I was embarrassed to even be in the same room with it. I said, "Uh—"

"Come on, come on! It should fit you perfectly! Then I'll put mine on and we can go wander around the Spacer Sector and show off!"

"Look," I said. "I don't think so. I mean, I used to wear the real thing, you know?"

She kept smiling. "So?"

"So, it just isn't what I want to do. I mean, Deadtowners can be assholes, but they don't deserve to—" I broke off, realizing I was on the verge of calling her *rich* again.

Still smiling, she said, "I've got two shops who are dying for me to make more of these. Like—what's your problem?"

I took a deep breath. "I think it stinks to make money off other people's poverty. I mean, that's taking it too far, Blackie."

Her face seemed to freeze into place. She was still holding the fake rag-wraps out, like she hadn't heard me. I started to pull my clothes back on.

"You make me sick," she said.

I should have kept my mouth shut. Instead I said, "Yeah, well I'm still not going to wear your little poser outfit."

I felt the storm coming before it actually hit, and I had just enough time to think "oops." Then Blackie hit me with a rain of fists.

"I am not a goddam poser!!" she shrieked. *"I-am-not-a-goddam-poser!!!"*

I took it for a few seconds because I was so overwhelmed—long enough to be pounded up against a wall. I could feel her satisfaction with every blow she connected, and it began to occur to me that she really didn't like me very much. Then I calculated a blow to her jaw and laid her flat.

If she hadn't eaten so many stims, she'd have been out cold. As it was, she just lay there and gazed at the ceiling. I pulled on the rest of my clothes and my wig, and headed for the front door. On the way out I passed the last of the semi-conscious Deadtowners sprawled in her living room. I almost told them what she's planning to sell to the fancy boutiques, but I guess they'll find out on their own soon enough.

I didn't think about moving out even then. Can you believe it? It still hadn't sunk in. I was so used to the storms and lulls of Blackie, I thought what had just happened was more of the usual.

I walked, knowing my course would take me to the fast-food stalls and not wanting to go there, but not really having the energy or the imagination to think of anything else to do. I couldn't go to the Salvation Army, and I didn't want to show up at the pits often enough to give the Q'rin a chance to recognize me. And I guess I was lonely. I still had some money left from last pay day. It would be weird to actually pay for food instead of stealing.

At first glance everything looked like it has for the past two years. Skids hanging around near the trash, government workers and tinkers stuffing their faces, Deadtowners and dogs cruising. But everyone was human. Even the Skids. The dogs and tinkers were acting all buddy-buddy, and the G-workers were grinning nervously at them both. It was creepy. Like accidently stumbling into an Earth Klan rally.

I ordered a sub and sat down, automatically putting half of it aside for Deadtowners. Never thought I'd be on this end of the transaction. Then I heard a voice.

"Hey Shade! What're you sitting by yourself for, girl?"

It was a tinker named Bill, a guy about my age. He's not bad, I guess. I see him around Mr. Field's office a lot. He was smiling and waving me over to where he was sitting with six other tinkers.

I got up and moved over there like a zombie. I was sure all the Deadtowners were watching me play the traitor, but they only had eyes for the half-sub I'd left behind. Maybe they didn't know who I was anymore.

"How ya doing, sexy?" Bill said, only half-joking.

"Okay I guess. You come from the casinos?"

They had. I listened to a bunch of nonsense about how they'd won this much and lost that much. My sandwich tasted like plasti-fix. I felt like the most *alien* alien in the universe.

"You feeling okay?" Bill asked.

"My roommate had a loud party last night."

One of the middle-aged tinkers grinned at me. "You should have made her share him with you," he said, but his eyes were disinterested as he scanned my body.

I let that one pass. As soon as they realized I wasn't going to be any fun, they ignored me.

"I hear Field is going to work for the fucking Q'rin," the middle-aged guy said to Bill.

Bill shrugged. "Can't say. He hasn't said anything about it."

"Don't give me that shit, kid. If I've heard rumors, you sure have. He's gonna help them tear down half of fucking Deadtown."

"So what?"

"I'll tell you what. If we don't get the army in here those fucking Q'rinniggers are gonna own this planet."

"No way," I said, without thinking first.

"Huh?"

"No way is Earth going to send a military force to this sleazy, backwater planet. We don't even have a real police force. That's why all the dogs are ex-tinkers. Just a bunch of hired thugs."

"She's right," said Bill. "Best you can hope for on this planet is to keep your head above water. Don't mess with politics."

Everyone agreed with that except the middle-aged guy. They were all thinking about the money they were going to make and trying *not* to think about who's going to be giving it to them.

"Long as they stay on their side of town," the middle-aged guy said. "Yeah. Ugly bastards. I hear they made the Aesopians out of household pets. That's why they hang around together."

"The Aesopians made themselves," I said. God only knows why I bothered.

He glared at me. "Shut up, bitch."

"No one knows what they originally looked like," I lectured. "They worshipped animals for thousands of years. When their technology was advanced enough, they started playing with their genes, trying to imitate the characteristics of their gods."

"Who the fuck cares?"

"They were more successful than they could have dreamed. Soon the different animal-types could not interbreed. Powerful families began to gain control, and war broke out between the groups. Lion, bear, elephant and wolf stuck together against horse, eagle, and cobra. The wars lasted hundreds of years and ravaged the planet. The survivors were thrown into a dark age."

"Jezuz, somebody shut her up!"

"I think it's a good story," said Bill. "You make that up, Shade?"

"A friend told me."

"So how come the Aesopians look like lions and bears and stuff?" Bill asked.

"I don't know. Maybe it was similar evolution. Maybe our two planets were seeded by the same original race."

"You queer for them or something?" said Middle-age.

"When the Aesopians finally rose to technological heights again, they vowed never to fight among themselves. They're proud of their forms.

That's why they accept the name *Aesopian* from humans. Because of the talking animals."

"It's their fault we lost the Ragnir war," the middle-aged guy said.

I bet he wouldn't say that to Knossos's face. I bet he didn't even fight in it. Lots of non-vets have loud opinions.

I was getting depressed, so I stopped talking about it. "See you Monday," I said to Bill. The other guys said goodbye too, but I couldn't remember their names.

I walked around for a long time, thinking about Knossos and Mr. Field. I keep forgetting that Knossos doesn't like me anymore. Maybe Mr. Field will stop liking me once he gets to know me better.

My walk took me past the Baby School.

I haven't seen any major new Baby houses in Deadtown. I bet the chicken hawks, who kept small stables in-house, are doing record business. The independent kids are probably too scared to come out yet.

I couldn't stop looking at the boarded-up door. I wondered if the bodies were still inside. I couldn't smell anything special.

I don't know why I went in. Maybe I just wanted to see for myself that they were gone. Maybe I wanted to remind myself what money really buys. I went in through the same bolt-hole Ramona had shown me that first time.

Her coloring book was still on the bed. Next to it was a burned spot that went all the way to the floor.

The Q'rin-dogs must have had their force guns turned up to full blast. But it still takes three or four shots to completely vaporize a body. There were burns and char marks all over the place. A trail of blood led into the kitchen.

But it was fresh.

I didn't recognize Stone at first. The right side of his body is badly burned and festering. He's so skinny now that his bones are sticking out through some of the burned places. He was on the floor trying to reach the water in the sink when I found him. When he saw me, he tried to crawl away. It was the look on what was left of his face that helped me realize who it was.

I carried him to one of the beds. He must have hurt bad, but he didn't make a sound.

"How did you get away?" I asked him.

"Bolt-hole. I almost made it—but not fast enough. Water . . ."

I got him some fresh water. When he drank some, he coughed it up again. It was red. Crawling back and forth between the kitchen and the bolt-hole must have torn him up even more inside.

"Lilo," he whispered.

"What?"

His good eye focused on me and glared. I had caught him grieving for his friend.

"I said Lyrri. That Lyrri-dog was here. I saw him looking around—maybe he thought you were killed."

"Good," I said. "Did he come with the Q'rin?"

"No. Later."

He tried more water. This time he just barely wet his lips with it.

"Remember the first time he talked to you and Lilo? How come he knew you knew me?" I should have just left him alone, but something was uncoiling in my guts.

"My pimp told him."

"Your pimp? Someone sets you up with the Lyrri? You're crazy! They could kill you!"

"She doesn't care."

I think I knew then, but I had to hear it.

"Who, Stone?"

"Blackie."

All this time I had thought she was just like her mom. But she was really just like her dad.

"Stone, do you know a black-skinned, brown-eyed kid—curly hair, about ten, called himself Farouk?"

He laughed. I wish he hadn't.

"The Lyrri love Babies. That's how she makes her living. That's how I . . ."

More water. I don't think it helped. Then he fell asleep sitting up. I put what was left of a blanket over him and put the water where he could reach it. Then I went out and scored some numbrain. Nice dig dose. He won't feel anything for awhile.

Blackie had company when I went back. I stood on the fire escape and listened.

"She likes you," Blackie was saying. "She thinks you're—just—really sexy."

"How wonderful," said Chaz. "When will she come back?"

"Pretty soon," said Blackie. "She has to work tomorrow."

So she knows. Maybe she read my notebook. I've been a complete asshole.

I climbed up to my floor and got this notebook. Then I crawled down again. I couldn't resist hearing what she had to say to her best customer. She was rambling.

"Like, don't get mad if she's polite but curt, okay? I mean, she acts like it's no big deal, but it's important to me. Whatever the reason, it makes me feel really bad. Like, we just end up saying things we don't mean. I guess I'll always be happy we shared friendship and happier times. Just because I might never see her again doesn't mean she can stop being my friend."

I wonder if that's what she said when she sold Farouk.

I came back here, scoring more numbrain on the way. I wonder if I could get Stone to a doctor without killing him on the way? I'm almost out of money. Maybe Mr. Field will help.

Stone woke up moaning, so I gave him the rest of the numbrain. That'll last another six hours. I'd better go score some more, and try to call Mr. Field. If I can't do that, I'm gonna carry Stone on the damn transport myself.

When I got back, Stone was dead. There was a knife in his hand, and his throat was cut. But the knife was in his *burned* hand. The one he could barely move.

I just ran. That was last night. It's almost night again.

I went to the warehouse where Knossos had been last week, and of course it was empty. I don't know if I expected that or not. I crawled into the vent in the floor so I can have another escape route if Chaz comes. I slept for a while, but I had a bad dream.

I was back in my room at Blackie's place. I had gone back to get my notebook. I could hear Blackie and Chaz talking downstairs. I picked up the notebook, but then I thought I should get some clothes too. So I snuck downstairs and raided Blackie's closet. And then I wanted some food, so

I snuck into the kitchen. And the two of them walked in there to find me with my hands full of junk.

Just before I woke up I dreamed that swamp rats were crawling up this vent toward me.

I had thought I wouldn't feel sleepy or hungry after what happened to Stone. But I am. Thoughts of submarine sandwiches are almost pushing out the images of that burned face.

He was just such a tough bastard. He wouldn't scream when customers tortured him, and he wouldn't lie down and die even after his body was ruined. Maybe he might have killed himself out of shame for accepting help from me. He had a lot of pride, even for a Scarbaby.

Doesn't seem to matter where I go or what I do. The flesh eaters are everywhere.

I had tried to phone Mr. Field when Stone was still alive, but he was out. I told his wife who I was. That was a mistake. Once she realized I was an employee, she couldn't even bring herself to be civil to me. I told her it was an emergency, and she wanted to know what about. Wouldn't give the number where he was.

I've got one thing I could maybe do. I could go to Donokh. I keep his card inside this notebook. I could use it. The hungrier I get, the more I think about that. I also keep having thoughts of Chaz crawling up this vent toward me like the swamp rats. Every noise I hear makes my heart stop.

I just hope Donokh doesn't decide he owns me.

I rode the transport two stops past the pits, right into Fortressland. I swear, even the shops look like they were built to withstand a siege. I was nervous. When Donokh was chasing me I felt self-assured, but now I feel like a beggar.

The transport let me off right outside the main complex. Its bulk loomed over me like some alien city in an old comic book. It was beautiful, in a military sort of way, but it was anything but welcoming.

I could see the Q'rin-dogs eyeing me as I walked up to the first gate, but I was careful not to look directly at anyone. No one spoke to me. One of the guys at the gate took my card and then stared at me for the longest time, looking like he was thinking, *What the hell is this supposed to be?* But he just grunted, handed me back the card, opened the gate, and gave me a little shove.

The guys at the second gate let me through without a hitch, and the guy at the third gate was almost cheerful. "You'll have to walk all the way to the rear of the complex, then go east," he said. "It's a long way, and you'll have to ask more specific directions when you get closer."

So I walked. Have to admit it was interesting. The main avenue was full of people, and I saw a lot more Q'rin women. Some of them even work as dogs. You don't see many lady-dogs on the human side of town—especially those of the Q'rin persuasion—so I was surprised to see so many here. I'm not sure what to make of it. Q'rin women are hardly what I could call frail, yet their men seem so protective.

I walked past a lot of reflective-type windows. I wondered if people were watching me from the inside.

After about an hour, I came to the rear of the complex and turned east. Asked the first guy I saw for directions to Donokh's quarters. He told me, then walked me partway so I wouldn't get lost.

"Just put your card in the slot by the door," he said. "That will get you in."

I could feel him checking me out as I walked away. Reminded me of what was probably going to happen at Donokh's place. I wasn't sure if I was more frightened or curious.

When I found what I hoped was the place, I slipped the card in a slot. It spat back out at me and the door opened.

Donokh's place is snazzy, but only by Q'rin standards. He wasn't home. I just stood in the front room until the tension wore off, then went looking. I called his name. Didn't want to catch him on the toilet or anything. That wouldn't be a real great start.

Once I was sure he wasn't there, I hid this notebook behind a sort of couch thing in the front room. Then I went looking for food. But I just can't figure out half the stuff in this apartment. So I went into the sleeping quarters and curled up on the bed. I pulled off the blonde wig and my shades, and went to sleep.

I woke up with his hand on my shoulder. I looked at him just long enough to determine that he was happy to see me there, and said, "I'm hungry."

"Yes," he said, sitting down on the bed. "What happened to your job with Field?"

Everything came back to me in a rush. I was amazed that I could have forgotten Stone's face even for a moment.

"A Lyrri is after me. Since before I met you. He's killed two of my friends."

"What Lyrri?"

"Chaz."

He put his big hand on the side of my face. "Tell me everything," he said.

I did, except for the part about Knossos and the warehouse.

"You can stay here with me," he said. "But I can't kill him for you."

"I know that. I was just hoping maybe he'd get tired of chasing me."

"He hasn't yet."

"Yeah, but that's because Blackie told him I think he's sexy. She probably kept putting him off with promises thật she was working on me. Then she gave him Farouk to keep him busy."

"What about Field?"

"Chaz knows I was working there. He probably knows about you, too; but at least if he knows about you he won't think I think he's sexy anymore."

"Do you think I'm sexy?"

"If I say yes, am I going to have to wait two hours before we eat?"

He laughed. As Q'rin laughs go, it was pretty hearty. Then he kissed me. Made me feel hot and dirty, like a kiss should.

"I wouldn't want your mind to be on anything but me," he said. "We'll eat first."

Of course I knew what the deal would be if I stayed with him. And part of the reason I wanted to eat first was that I was a little scared. But after several months of celibacy, I was so horny I could hardly stand it; and once we had started eating I found out I wasn't as hungry as I had thought. He kept giving me those hot looks, touching my knee and my hair. I ate until the edge was off my hunger, and I said, "Look, it turns out you're more of a distraction than my stomach is." Then I slithered into his lap and kissed him.

He stood up with me still in his arms and

carried me into the bedroom. I let him undress me without helping him, because he really seemed to want it that way. He exposed my little breasts and stroked them with his big hands.

"Come be my little street urchin," he said.

"All right. Am I under arrest?"

So we played the Q'rin warrior and his captive girl for a while. But he was very gentle with me. He stripped off his clothes in record time, uncovering a first-class body. His skin was smooth and tasted spicy, and he kissed me all over like I was the most scrumptious thing he'd ever tasted. Before long I was feeling that other hunger, the slippery kind.

He has the biggest penis I've ever seen. It took me a while to get used to it, but it was worth it. Afterward he held me and talked to me in soft tones.

"You're beautiful," he said.

"So are you," I said, meaning it. I love that rocky face of his, and that big body that makes me feel so delicate. I've never felt that way before in my life.

Eventually my stomach started talking to me again, but I ignored it. I didn't want him to think I was only there for the food. He was the one who suggested we finish supper.

Now he's on patrol, so I can scribble in peace.

"You'll be safe anywhere in the compound," he told me. "Outside, I can't guarantee anything. Just remember to take your card with you."

Maybe later I'll explore the place. For now I think I'm just going to sleep. Might as well take advantage of the safety while I can.

I dreamed I went out into Donokh's front room and found Stone sitting there, his face still burned and his neck bloody.

"I want to live here, too," he said.

"We'll find you a better place," I said, really meaning "I don't want you here."

As if he had heard my thought, the wound in his neck reopened. I tried to make it close with sheer force of will. It didn't work, so I pretended it had anyway.

I saw Donokh outside and got scared.

"Go into the bathroom and I'll get you numbrain," I said. He went, but he left red stains and chunks of burned flesh where he'd been sitting. I tried to clean it up. My face was all twisted in guilt and embarrassment. When Donokh finally came in I tried to relax my expression, but half my face wouldn't cooperate. I reached up and felt burned and twisted flesh.

The first thing I did when I woke up was touch my face. It felt smooth. But I was so upset I didn't want to sleep anymore, so I took a walk. Funny, the dogs who killed the Babies are in here somewhere, but I feel safer in here than I did outside.

I just kind of wandered around, looking at people and scenery all afternoon. The Q'rin were looking back at me with a "what's so great about you" look on their faces, not as an insult but in honest curiosity. They knew I wouldn't be inside their fortress unless there was something special about me. It was a rare opportunity, to be there as a guest, and I drank in the sights and sounds—those rocky people in their stone and iron buildings, all angles and squares.

But some of the gardens I glimpsed showed me they understand beauty, too. The courtesans lounged there in their silks and perfumes, like alien flowers. I didn't get too close to them, though. I don't think they like me.

Finally I saw some women working out in one of the courtyards. These women looked like pit fighters, not clerks or dogs or courtesans—or whatever else women do in here. I sat and watched them for awhile. Good stuff.

Now that I'm used to them, I just can't see why some human men say they're ugly. You just have to look at them differently. I bet the Cubists and the Surrealists of the early twentieth century would have loved to have them as models. And those twenty-first century guys, the Cyberrealists.

They train hard. No human athlete could take that kind of abuse. But watching them is like watching a ballet. I guess that's how I feel about the pits. Winning money is important, but it's the moves that count with me.

Larissa's here, too. Don't know why that surprised me. She came out with some of the men who sat with Mr. Field and me in Oshrii's box. She had several practise matches with both men and women. That takes guts. She beat them all. She has the reach, and Deadtown trains knife fighters better than anything. I still carry three of my favorite knives where I can get at them.

During her break she came over to talk to me.

"So another Deadtowner bites the dust, huh, Shade?"

"Every day. When was the last time you went back?"

"Haven't set foot in Deadtown since Oshrii took over my career." She grinned at me. "I'm a survivor. It would be stupid to go back."

"Have you made enough money to get off this planet yet?"

"Did that a long time ago."

I couldn't believe my ears. "Then what are you still doing here?"

"You know anywhere else a knife fighter can make a living? I've got my own place here. I've got respect. I've got a good lover." She nodded to Oshrii's second. He was watching us with curiosity.

"I grew up on Hook," she said. "Military brat. If I hadn't run away from my old man, I probably would have joined the Service. I like the action."

I snuck a glance at the place her right ear should have been. For some reason, the sight depressed me.

"I notice you've moved in with Donokh," she said. "You have good taste."

Well, at least she's one human I don't have to explain my taste in men to. When she went back to talk to her lover, I could see the sparks between them. I guess she really is happy.

But I just feel confused. On the way back, I scoped the people I passed, and I'm not sure how I feel about what I saw. They all knew me. And they all expect me to stay. I guess I should be flattered.

When Donokh came home, I didn't know if I wanted to jump on him or tell him goodbye.

"You're restless," he said. He went over to one of his gizmos and slipped a disc into it. Music came out.

"Hey, that's Mary Chocholak!" I said. "I used to listen to her back in Hollywood."

"Making music and painting pictures are two of the three things humans do best," he said.

Well, that solved my indecision.

Later, I could tell he was thinking about my problem with Chaz.

"Why do you think Chaz really wants you?" he asked me.

"He wants to torture me. He's a Lyrri, isn't he?"

"We Q'rin knew the Lyrri long before you humans did. You made them the monsters they are today. You showed them new vices they would not have thought of on their own."

"Huh?"

"You gave them something to do. They would have died of boredom without you."

"What are you talking about?"

"The Lyrri are the oldest known race in the galaxy. We others knew enough not to tamper with them. We didn't ask them what they thought, how they felt. We didn't want to make love to them. You humans came along and ruined everything. You woke them up."

"That's not what I heard!"

"Of course not."

"It's not all our fault!"

"Why do you think Chaz is after you?"

"I didn't do anything. He couldn't have thought I wanted him. All I do is run away from him."

"You said he sent you a message once, about *business*."

I hadn't told him about this notebook. I nodded.

"When you bet with Lord Oshrii the other day, you won every match."

"Almost."

"When you bet with the Special One, weeks ago, you won every match."

"Yes."

"When you bet with the elephant man—"

"Yes!"

"Why?"

"Because—I just do. I can tell what people are going to do sometimes."

"What am I going to do now?"

I scoped him. "You want to make love again."

He looked shocked, then laughed. "Yes. All this arguing is getting me excited. But I'll wait. I want you to come for a walk with me."

I was nervous now. Should I let him know how good I am? My skill would be very useful to him. I should have kept it to myself, but he would have known I was lying to him. If I held back, he could turn into an enemy. Either way, I would become a prisoner.

We got dressed and went outside. He asked me questions about the people we passed. I told him about half of what I could scope. That's no solution, but I didn't know what else to do. He suspected I was holding back, but he was uncertain. So we're even. Almost.

"You tell me something now," I said. "Tell me why you're going to build a fortress in Deadtown."

That was a hard one for him. I thought his eyes were going to poke holes through me while he decided what to tell me.

"*I* am not building a fortress," he said. "Oshrii and his allies are."

"What's the split over?"

"The Lyrri, for one thing. They are unsurpassed in the art of extracting information. Oshrii calls them The Lords of Torture. Some of us don't want that kind of contact with the Lyrri. We feel they could be making the same mistake you humans did.

"The Lyrri are leaving their planet in greater numbers than ever, now. They have technology we never dreamed of. We are divided about what we should do."

And those dumb tinkers think it's about whose neighborhood is whose in Deadtown.

"What about the Aesopians?" I asked.

"We can't have trouble from them now."

Good thing I didn't tell him what I saw Knossos and his pals doing.

We went back to his place and sat around thinking about heavy stuff. Finally he asked me, "Why didn't you ever try your hand at pit fighting? Your ability could have helped you a lot, there."

"I'm not tough enough."

He laughed so hard—for a Q'rin, anyway—it scared me. Then he grabbed me and started pulling my clothes off. I guess we had reached an agreement.

Today they brought Knossos in. I was watching Larissa train when ten dogs and Donokh marched him in through the third gate. His hands weren't cuffed or anything—I'm not sure they have cuffs that big—and he seemed as self-composed as always. He looked at me as he went past. My heart almost stopped.

You can bet Larissa's boyfriend found a fast excuse to disappear. Things are going to get lively now. Did they catch Knossos hoarding weapons? Did they arrest him as he was paying off his debt? They didn't bring anyone else in. Are the others dead?

Why do I care? They don't care what happens to me.

I'll try to find out what's going on through Donokh. If I ever see him. Everyone got very tense when Knossos came through. You could see where the line is drawn in here. Larissa and I are on opposite sides. Story of my life.

Donokh could come in any minute now, so I'd better hide this thing again.

Donokh never came home. But after I went to bed, Larissa's boyfriend came knocking on the door.

He brought two other aides with him. He gave me a bland smile and said, "I am Hazaar. Please get dressed and come with me."

"What if I say no?"

"Please do not say no."

I glanced at my nightgown—one of Donokh's tunics—and tried to look embarrassed and submissive.

"Okay," I mumbled, turned my back, then swung around and slammed the door in their faces. Donokh had made sure I knew how to lock it the first night we spent together, and I didn't waste any time. He had also warned me that thirty or forty force gun blasts could get through the metal. But I had a feeling these men weren't willing to declare open war yet.

The com buzzed. For the hell of it, I answered.

"Unlock the door," Hazaar commanded.

"No. Go away."

"You can't stay in there forever."

"You don't have that fortress built yet," I said.

"No. But the fortress is a formality. Wouldn't you rather be on the winning side?"

"Not as a hostage."

"You're a hostage now. A hostage to outdated and bigoted beliefs. You could do better in your choice of patrons."

Why was he telling me this? What difference does it make to Oshrii what Donokh's little slut thinks? Even if I did hang around with the elephant man once.

"You don't need to talk to me," I said. "I don't know anything about the elephant man that you don't know. In fact, you know more."

"That's not the issue," he said.

"Then what is?"

"Think about it," he said, then they went away.

So after all this time on Z'taruh it's finally occured to me that people might want more from me than my ass or my pain. That must sound pretty stupid, right? Because isn't it obvious? The way politics work around here, it's good to know what your enemies might do. I've never made my ability that much of a secret. I've even rented it out from time to time.

But whatever it may look like, I can't read minds like you would read a book. And I'm not that much better at scoping than a lot of people here. In fact, Oshrii's better than me. And Knossos is more brilliant. And Chaz—

Who-the-fuck-knows what he really wants.

The thing is, I could have played the people on the Hill just like I played people back in Hollywood. I could have lived well, once I figured it all out. Or I could have haunted the poker dens until I had enough to leave Z'taruh and go to Hook, the con capital of the galaxy.

I know that now. I didn't know it before. And now, none of those possibilities is enough. Because I don't want to be stuck with this life forever.

I guess my little encounter with Oshrii's dogs is wearing off. I don't need to scribble down a bunch of crazy ideas now. I can get something to drink and try to get back to sleep. When Donokh comes in I'll tell him what happened and what I think. Most of it, anyway. I wonder what he'll say.

*   *   *

A few hours later, Donokh called me on his private line.

"Tomorrow there will be a public hearing," he said. "I don't think you'll need to fear any kidnapping attempts from Oshrii by then. But keep the door locked for the rest of the night."

"A *public* hearing? For Knossos?"

"Yes."

"What are you charging him with?"

"For existing without obvious means of support."

"For vagrancy! Half the population of Capital is guilty of that!"

"You're trying my patience."

"Well, excuse me. I call 'em as I see 'em."

"I'll call you tomorrow for the hearing," he said.

I guess we've had our first fight.

The next day I was out with everyone else for the hearing. It was held in a big courtyard behind the complex. There was quite a turnout just to see a vagrant. When they brought Knossos out, he looked at me again, and I got the definite feeling he was trying to tell me something. He looked calm though, and he stood there like a king under the glare of his enemies.

Damned if the whole thing wasn't conducted in the Q'rin language. If Larissa hadn't been sitting next to me, I might have missed the high points.

"Hey," she said as she sat down. "No hard feelings about last night?"

"Not toward you," I said.

"Good. No need to explain politics to a Deadtowner, because she already knows the score."

"Don't worry about it," I said. I was hoping

she could translate for me. She did, as well as she could.

A council of eight noblemen sat down on some stone benches, facing the crowd. Knossos stood facing them, his back to us. Oshrii was the only judge I recognized.

"You are charged with vagrancy. What is your plea?"

"I, Knossos of clan Knossos, Lord of Ships of the Ragnir War and the War of Three Worlds, have lived, as well as I can with no money and no ties with my homeworld, on Z'taruh for the last ten years."

"And what have you done for these last ten years, *ex*-Lord Knossos?" Oshrii asked him.

"I have endeavored to live with honor and justice," said Knossos.

"And how do honor and justice survive in a man who steals the clothing he wears and eats from refuse bins?" said Oshrii.

Despite my hurt feelings, that last part really made me furious. Knossos never did those things. But he just said, "I live in humble circumstances, but I cannot unlearn virtue. I practise it more faithfully than ever your Lyrri allies could."

Some of the judges frowned at that, but others nodded their approval.

"Lord Knossos," one of the latter said, "are you conspiring to cause revolt on this planet?"

"No."

"How can you say that when you have been seen with members of your old crew?"

"Who else would I associate with on a planet of strangers?"

"I suppose the real question is what, in your mind, constitutes *association*; and whether it violates our laws."

"My Lords," said Knossos, as if he were speaking to equals, "the question before you today is not whether or not I am a revolutionary. If you had evidence of that, I would not be standing before you now; I would be in a Questioning Cell or with the Lords of Torture. Today I am accused of being a vagrant. You must decide that I am or I am not."

The crowd really got into that. There was even some scattered applause. Once again, the line was clearly drawn between the pro-Lyrri and the anti-Lyrri.

The Lords began to argue. Oshrii was studying the others the same way I was. He could see they were leaning toward dismissal. Finally he said something only the other judges and Knossos could hear.

"Very well," he said finally. "We find you guilty of vagrancy. You are fined fifty Z'taruhn dollars or three months in prison."

"My Lords," said Knossos, "you know that I have no money. And three months is far longer than the mandatory sentence for vagrancy."

"As I'm sure you know from long experience," said Oshrii. "Nevertheless, that is our decision."

A couple of the judges seemed uncomfortable with that, but no one disagreed. I guess even the anti-Lyrri Lords are nervous about having Knossos at large.

"Larissa," I said. "Loan me two credits, will you?"

Now was the time we would see if she was really still a Deadtowner or if she had turned into Oshrii's creature. She was quiet for a moment while Knossos argued with the Lords.

"Is three months to be the mandatory sentence

from now on? Will you feed and house every vagrant on Z'taruh for three months apiece?"

"No," said Oshrii. "Only the Aesopians."

Larissa told me that last part as she stuffed two credits into my hand. Maybe that bit of arrogance from Oshrii is what helped her make up her mind. I ran up the aisle and right up to Knossos.

"This man loaned me fifty credits when I was broke," I announced in a loud voice. "Now I'm paying it back."

I gave Knossos my last forty-eight credits and Larissa's two. Then he said something to me in a voice only I could have heard:

"Shade, get out of this compound as soon as you possibly can."

I must have gone white as a sheet. Oshrii smiled at me.

"Sit down," one of the judges said.

On the way back to my seat I glanced at Oshrii. He was still smiling at me, almost as if he were pleased. But I knew better.

Knossos paid his fine and they released him. I waited until I was sure he was safely out the gate, then went back to Donokh's place and locked the door. I had no idea what I was going to do. Knossos might think I was safer outside, but he didn't know about Chaz.

After a while, Donokh came home.

"You should not have interfered," he said.

"You know what would have happened to Knossos in prison," I said. "And I don't think it would be to your advantage."

"I needed to speak with him alone!" he hissed. "I didn't get the chance last night, and I was going to try again today! I would have paid his fine myself!"

He looked like he was ready to shake me. I took a couple of steps backward. "Really?" I said.

He advanced on me, and this time he did take hold of my shoulders. "I can't set up a meeting outside the compound now, because Oshrii is watching too closely. You made yourself too obvious today!"

I couldn't think of anything to say to that. I just looked at him and hoped he wouldn't hurt me. He looked almost mad enough to.

Finally I said, "Do you want me to leave?"

His face got very still, except for a muscle near his jaw that jumped every few seconds, like he was gritting his teeth. I think even if I couldn't scope at all I would have known then that the answer was no. He didn't want me to leave, maybe not ever. He leaned down and kissed me a little harder than usual. Then he took hold of the neck of my shirt and tore it down the front, ripping it right off me.

"Hey," I said, "that was your shirt. If you want to destroy it, that's your business."

He picked me up and threw me over his shoulder, just like a character in one of those *War Lust* vids, only it wasn't that much fun. He threw me on the bed and glared down at me, still mad enough to hurt.

I rolled up into a little ball and tried to shut him out. This was too much. This wasn't what I liked at all. After a while I felt his hands on my back, stroking me like I was made of glass and he was afraid I would break.

"I'm sorry," he said. "I'm sorry, Shade. I won't hurt you. Please look at me."

He just kept stroking until I unwound and turned to face him. All the anger was gone from his eyes, but he still looked worried. He kept stroking me, as if to prove he wasn't going to hurt me. He pulled off the rest of my clothes, and then his own, and made love to me like he was afraid it might be the last time. Then he did it again.

"I know I made a mistake," I said. "But I didn't think I had any other choice. I can't read minds."

He was lying on top of me by then, still inside me. "Can't you?" he whispered.

"No. I swear I can't."

"All right." He kissed my earlobe. "Would you mind if we did it one more time?"

"I don't mind," I said, "as long as I can get on top this time."

We rolled over, and proceeded to show him that I cared very much for him, too. He needed to know.

I keep having this stupid feeling that Knossos got himself arrested just so he could warn me. I wish I didn't have those feelings. It hurts so much to find out how wrong they are.

But with Donokh treating me like he's afraid he's going to lose me, it may hurt a lot more to find out those feelings are right.

I dreamed about Stone again. He didn't say anything, but I got the feeling he was trying to warn me. I woke up to find Donokh gone again. He's been gone more and more lately.

Just now I glanced up from writing this and saw some people walking past the window.

They were Lyrri. I've got to get out of here.

After Donokh left for the day, I walked out the front gate. As I was leaving, at least twenty Lyrri were coming in. Chaz wasn't among them. I turned a corner and ran and ran. And ran.

Now I'm sitting with some Skids. Dirt and junk from the garbage bins is rapidly covering me. I'll bet in a few days no one could recognize me. Will it be enough?

I feel bad about leaving Donokh without saying goodbye. But I can't be his prisoner any more than I could be Blackie's or Oshrii's. He'd have to lock me up just to keep me safe.

No one here cares if I scribble in this notebook. They just keep talking to themselves.

Maybe I belong here after all.

Now I know how come Skids can sit in alleys all day and night without getting tired of it. It's because of this stuff they call meltdown. They make it from one of the swamp plants. To give you an idea, a more refined version of meltdown is numbrain. You can get the plants anywhere and make meltdown in a couple of hours. It's the refinement process that makes numbrain expensive. Skids will even brave swamp rats to get the plants.

Good thing Skids don't like loki, or they'd have to brave a lot more than swamp rats.

Some generous old guy gave me some of his meltdown in exchange for just sitting and listening to him. After awhile we were both so melted it got downright surrealistic. We talked about shit that wouldn't make any sense now. That was yesterday, and I'm still glued to the same spot. He went away when he forgot who I was and what he wanted to talk to me about. Wonder if he's a vet or some other throwaway.

I can hardly feel my butt at all, and the

meltdown has killed my hunger. Maybe later I'll check out that shelter in Midtown Mr. Field told me about. Or maybe I'll just sit and watch the world go by.

I bet everyone in Capital eventually walks past this spot. Or maybe it just seems that way. Thought I saw Blackie today. She wouldn't recognize me though, because I've turned my face into a mask. I'm a different woman. I'm old and wrinkled, and my tits hang down. What there is of them. My hair is white with ash.

We all eat from the garbage can, though we don't always know it. We all sleep in the alley. We all try to block it out with drugs. Once we lived in the jungle with the other sane people. We traded it all for flush toilets and force guns. Then it all comes apart when your checkbook doesn't balance.

But I'm lying. I really love this shit. I just wonder sometimes if Knossos's people changed themselves because they almost turned into what we are.

There was a bear man in my alley too. He wasn't drinking or anything, and at first I thought he might be Rorra the wrestler. But he was older, and his ears were all chewed up. "I've come to say goodbye," he told everyone. "Are you leaving?" they asked him. "Where are you going?"

"I don't know," he said. "I've been dreaming of Home."

I wanted to ask him what he saw in his dreams, but I'm shy around most Aesopians. And ashamed of the way other humans talk about them. No one has the guts to say things to their faces, but they're treated like undesirables. All because looking at them makes us remember how we backed out on them in the war.

This bear man was reminding me of a song I heard when I was a kid. Something like, don't go into the woods today because the bears are dancing or having a picnic or something. Or the bear went into the woods or did something. I thought and thought about it, but I couldn't figure it out.

Other Aesopians wander past there from time to time—bear and lion and wolf men, mostly. I still jump inside a little when I see them, with their fur and claws and teeth, their three-fingered hands and mobile lips. I want to ask them if they've dreamed about Home, but it isn't my business now.

No elephant man is here yet. I'm not even looking anymore.

No one knows me. They think I'm some Runaway who skidded out without hitting any of the stages inbetween. I'm getting into that. I can almost believe it myself. Maybe if I can turn into that other woman, all of Shade's enemies will go away.

Another warm night, just like all the warm days all year 'round. Almost out of light. Still not hungry. Maybe tomorrow.

I went to the shelter in Midtown. Walked for ten blocks before my butt woke up. Walked for fifteen before I realized I'd lost my shades. Stole a pair off a Runaway. He said it was okay as long as I left him alone.

They had muffins along with the gruel. Good stuff, lots of fiber. Now we can all shit with confidence.

I drank some coffee and amused myself by wondering what everyone would look like if they were all cleaned up and wearing fancy clothes. I

was just kidding at first, but soon I was taking it
very seriously. I saw bankers and college profes-
sors, art investors and businessmen. Politicians.
Vid-stars. When I caught myself making up stories about them, I stopped. That's a little too
crazy.

Shelters are like spaceports. Or airports. Or
tran stations, whatever you want. People are pass-
ing through, confused, wondering if they're really ever going to get home. But I think it's okay
if this is my home for awhile. I really don't
mind. After I lost Hollywood and Mom, I stopped
expecting things to be nice. Besides, they have
loki and meltdown and numbrain here. We have
to hide it from the staff, but that's easy. Not very
many of them around.

So now I'm on an honest-to-God cot. Feels like
the alley. I don't care. I've got meltdown; took it
off some Skid who was sleeping and twitching on
the next cot. No one's gonna tell on me. I've got
my knives. No one cares anyway. Gonna lie back
and enjoy my drug.

Stone is sitting on my feet. Looking at me.
Wants my meltdown. Don't need it because he's
dead. Doesn't he know that? Told him where
Blackie lives. Maybe he'll go after her like a
revenge-zombie—eat her intestines. But no. He
just sits and stares at me.

Told him how she fucked me over. Told him
she was fucking Chaz. She's fucked. I guess I'm
just imagining him. Never saw him with my eyes
open before. Wonder how come I can sit up and
hold this pen so well. If it weren't for Stone and
the Skids in the other cots who are singing like
an angel choir—some tune that seems too beau-

tiful to be made up by my melted mind—I might think I was sober. But no, the choir sings on, and Stone is telling me volumes with the slightest twitch of his dead face.

He's a sad boy. Never had the things a boy should have. No toys or sweat socks. No underwear. He wishes he had it now. So do I.

Meltdown burnout. I'm starting to know it well. I woke up with my face pressed into this notebook. Got spiral marks branded into my cheek.

Guy in the next cot didn't wake up. Guess he couldn't take it. Wonder if the staff knows it yet. They'll know it when he starts to smell. Unless his body is so saturated with meltdown it's mummified.

Before they would let me have breakfast, they made me fill out a lot of papers about what kind of job I'm going to look for. I scribbled down a bunch of nonsense. Stuffed myself at breakfast, then out the door and time to waste. I heard them talking about how the meltdown stills are just a few blocks from the shelter. I went and watched them make some. Didn't take them long. Some Skids were selling pints of their blood so they could buy some. It's pretty cheap, even when someone else makes it for you, and there's a lot of it. I went to the blood shop and sold some of my own. No problem. I make it myself.

What an ordered life I'm living now.

I wandered past the fast-food stalls. No one looked at me twice. Or even once. I dug some tasty tidbits out of the trash and wandered on.

Lots of dogs around. They look nervous as hell. That's because the tinkers are splitting down the middle. Mr. Field must have started hiring. All the guys who aren't being picked or who can't stand the Q'rin are getting ugly. Think I'll have some meltdown and see if I can't sleep through the whole civil war.

Or even an interstellar war.

Stone has invited the dead guy from the next cot over here. Now they're both sitting on my feet. Hope they don't fart or anything.

The choir is getting bigger and louder. It rises and falls to the pulse beat in my temple. Making it hard to concentrate. Or write. Think I'll lie down and rest.

I missed breakfast. Have to go cruise my own. Feel like hell.

But they gave me some new clothes today. That was nice. They'll probably have to burn the old ones. Don't think I've ever been this dirty in my life.

One of my neighbors said something funny to me today. She said she'd been at the shelter a month, and she was ready to get out. But she must be crazy. She got here a few days after I did, and only a week or two has gone by. I haven't been sucking down that much meltdown. She said the administrator wanted to talk to me, so I got out of there as quick as I could. Wish those dumb volunteers would just leave me alone.

Something kind of scary: I ran into Snag today, and I was talking to him for twenty minutes or so before I remembered who he was. Must have still been hung over. He kept going, "Shade? Shade? Where are you living? What are you doing?" Don't remember what I said, but I don't think I told him anything.

He must've kept following me around though, because he showed up when I was trying to score at the meltdown stills. Knocked the bottle out of the man's hand just as he was about to hand it to me. "Poison!" he screamed. "Selling poison to children, you rat turd! You filthy vomit eater!"

The still man just shrugged and started pouring out meltdown for another customer. I yanked on his sleeve.

"Hey!" I said, "I didn't get mine!"

"Yours is on the ground. Lick it up if you want it."

"Motherfucker! C'mon, I paid for it! Give me mine!"

Snag was still talking to me, shaking my arm and trying to get my attention. But I didn't have time for him. Had to get my meltdown. Tried to talk to the still man, but he didn't care. Sometimes I forgot to be nice and called him motherfucker. No good.

When I finally gave up and looked for Snag, he was gone. I came back to the shelter and had supper.

So no meltdown tonight. Though it kinda feels like I still have it in my system. I can hear the choir. Wish they'd learn a new song.

Finally ran into the administrator when I was filling out the breakfast paperwork. I smiled at her, but she wasn't buying it.

"We don't bust our butts in here every day just so meltbrains like you can have a place to crash!"

"Bet you do," I said.

"Yeah. But not when we can help it. If you don't care enough about yourself to help your-

self, you can just go to hell. You're halfway there
already."

"Okay," I said. "I'll do better."

"Maybe you will, but you won't do it here. Get
out. I don't want to see your face in here again."

So I gathered up my few belongings and left.
Waited a couple of hours for the shift to change
and walked right back in again. Filled out the
papers under a new name. Got breakfast, got a
new cot, and went out to score some more
meltdown. Had to sell more blood, but that's
okay.

Gonna fly high tonight.

Still don't know if this happened or not, but I
think I was gang raped. Or maybe it was a dream.
Think I was trying to score more meltdown. I
was in an alley. I was outside, for sure, because I
saw concrete and big dumpsters. But I don't remember walking there or walking back. Just remember standing in line, staring at the still man.
Or was that yesterday? The still man always
looks the same. He dropped my bottle on the
pavement once and it broke, so I always hold on
real tight now.

Then I remember hanging over a dumpster
with my bare ass in the air and someone sticking
it to me. The bottom of the dumpster was a
hundred feet down, and it was empty. Dumpsters
are never empty around here. I could hear lots of
men's voices, and it just went on and on. I tried
to pull myself all the way into the dumpster.
Better to be in the garbage than have my ass out
there for the world to use.

I have lots of meltdown. Sometimes I care about
things and sometimes I don't. If I think about the

gang rape, I'm there again and feeling all those penises where they don't belong. Or I can be with Donokh and really get off. I can be in bed with him and feel everything, hear his voice. I want to go back there real bad and fuck him some more. He can lock me up or anything he wants.

I don't think the rape really happened, because I can see myself fucking Mr. Field, too. In his office on the big desk. I don't like to see that. It makes me feel bad.

I don't think the rape happened. I went into the bathroom and checked my vagina and my anus. They were dry and didn't have any sperm in them. Should have been gallons. And they should have been open a mile, so many penises went in there.

Sat on the dirty tile for a while and remembered my abortion. A hooker did it for me. Then she gave me some stuff to drink if it happens again. "Don't take chances," she said. "Drink this if you're even a day late. Don't let it get this far along again, or you'll have to come back and let me scrape it out for you."

Maybe she'll have to scrape a hundred babies out of me now. No sperm. Feels dry down there. I know I never fucked Mr. Field, but it seems as real as the gang rape. Wish I could just melt the whole idea out of my mind.

I don't know if the rape happened or not.

Went to score meltdown. Asked the still man did you fuck me? He said don't make me puke. Said did you see a bunch of guys rape me yesterday? Laughed and said meltdown dreams you imagined it. Tell me if you see me system president.

On the way home I'm saying still man for system president and sometimes people laughing sometimes not. Don't have to walk back and forth now just fly.

Choir is singing singing giving a headache. Can't write good. Just going to lie here and let it happen. I'm so happy.

So here I am in a new hidey-hole. I cruised the fast-food stalls just like the old days today, and did better than ever. It's taken two weeks to get the last of the meltdown out of my system. I still have a residual headache. At least I can remember stuff clearly now. Like I can remember my last night at the shelter.

I had a couple of hours of total bliss after drinking the meltdown. I was sure I had found nirvana. The choir sounded beautiful, and nothing in the galaxy could have frightened me or made me sad. After a while the choir got louder than I've ever heard them. I was sure I'd go deaf pretty soon. But I didn't fight it. Maybe I couldn't. I just let it sweep me up and wring my brain dry.

Eventually I felt a pressure on my feet. Stone and the dead bum. Only now they had Farouk with them. "Hey," I said, "shouldn't you guys be in Heaven or Purgatory or something?"

They kept motioning to someone over my shoulder. I couldn't see who it was. "Who's dead now?" I asked them. "Is it Blackie? Chaz? Donokh?"

The three of them smiled at me and pointed at the mysterious someone. She leaned over me and grinned. Took me a while to remember who she was.

She was me.

So when I could move again, sometime the next afternoon, I headed straight into the women's toilet and stripped my clothes off. Now that I was really awake, I checked myself for vaginal/anal damage and sperm—one more time. Didn't find any, so that's a load off my mind.

I scrubbed myself at the sink. Then I tore my clothes into strips and wrapped them around my body. I noticed how skinny I'd gotten. Meltdown isn't the most nutritious substance in the world.

I used one of my knives to hack my hair back into the proper style. When I looked in the mirror, I almost recognized myself again. I was ready to go find some plasti-fix and make myself some gear.

I walked out of the shelter with my back straight. It was like leaving prison. Smiled at the administrator on the way out and gave her the high sign. She watched me with her mouth open.

Chaz can just come find me, because I can't run anymore. If he gets me, he gets me. I'm not gonna let him kill me the way he killed Farouk.

I've been eating at the Salvation Army again. I even see Mira and Snag sometimes. They don't ask me any questions, and I return the favor.

Haven't seen Knossos yet. Guess he went back into hiding. I wonder when he's planning to leave. Probably best not to think about it.

My new hidey-hole is a good one. Funny, I feel safer than I have since before Chaz started chasing me.

*   *   *

I saw some old melthead friends of mine today. They didn't recognize me. They were too busy watching the still man. I never knew their names, but I don't think I would have said hello to them if I had. I remember how much good that did when I was one of them.

Some people look at me like they wonder when I'm going to go back. I don't mean Mira and Snag—they treat me like they always have. Just some people, like Jake, who I see around the food stalls sometimes. He looks real lean and angry these days, and he's not any friendlier than he's ever been.

"Hey," he told me today, "you belong in that still line, or you wouldn't have started with the stuff in the first place."

But I don't even crave meltdown anymore. It was like a place I hid. A mask I wore for awhile that almost smothered me. Sometimes when I look at the people standing around those stills I feel uncomfortable, because I know that's what I looked like.

Today I just wandered around the stalls, watching the way things have changed while I was chasing the meltdown. It's totally different from what it was the last time I paid any attention. For one thing, the tinkers are feuding. I've already seen two fist fights this morning (which gave me ample opportunity to plunder the tables while the combatants were occupied—scored one of those yummy meatball subs) and I expect to see more this afternoon.

"You work for the goddam *Q'rinniggers*, you're a nigger yourself!" one guy was screaming as fists flew. I think it pretty much summed up the sentiments of the tinkers who aren't working on the new Deadtown constructions. Yeah, it's money that's driving them apart. They say it's principles, but I've noticed people changing sides as soon as they get one of the new high-paying jobs. Or lose one. By the time Mr. Field is done hiring, over half the tinkers in Capital will be working for him, and the other half will be furious about it.

I sat down on one of the tables, after I had plundered lunch, and watched the people. This was another first, a Deadtowner actually being permitted to sit at one of the tables, because everyone is so divided they don't care about us right now. I saw other Deadtowners doing the same, resting their butts and wondering how to turn it all to their advantage. Saw Jake across the way and waved to him. He scowled back at me.

At the table next to mine, tinkers and Q'rin were actually eating together and talking. It was an amazing sight. Next to them was a table with Q'rin and Aesopians sitting together—not so unusual. But behind them some Q'rin and tinkers were sitting with Lyrri.

Nowhere did I see Aesopians and Lyrri sitting together. And I never will.

I haven't seen Donokh anywhere. I wonder where he's gone. I've caught a couple of glimpses of Oshrii, though not today. If I had, I wouldn't have been sitting out in the open like that, enjoying the politics despite myself and watching everyone split and reform, split and reform. I was getting some looks back, and I was proud I had rigged myself up properly with a plasti-fix vest and some dark red and brown rag-wraps. I don't have the money for a good haircut anymore, so I just hack at the mop with my knife, like a proper Deadtowner. I have a good pair of boots I stole from a drunk dog. That's all the human-dogs have to do with themselves lately—get drunk and swagger around like they're personally responsible for everyone in Capital.

"Shade?" I heard someone call. "Jesus, is that you?"

I looked and found Bill the tinker sitting with some Q'rin-dogs. He was looking at me like he was glad to see me, so I went over there.

I nodded to the Q'rin, who nodded back as they examined me with stony faces. "Hi there," I said to Bill. "How are you?"

"Fine," he said, looking at me with open dismay. "What happened to you?"

"Nothing," I said.

"When did you decide to become—I never knew you were a—is that your real hair?"

"I've always worn a lot of hats," I said. "Not to mention wigs. Right now I'm just being myself."

"Oh. Want some iced tea?" He offered from his own cup, so I accepted. "Field has been looking for you," he told me as I drank. "He's really been worried."

"Do me a favor and tell him I'm okay," I slurped. "And tell him I'll try to talk to him before—"

I couldn't remember how I had intended to end that sentence. I looked at the Q'rin who were sitting with Bill and listening so carefully to everything I was saying; then looked at the other tables with their various mixed occupants, at the armed dogs, and then finally at the Skids

and Deadtowners who were then being ignored
as if they didn't even exist anymore.

Before—?

Bill was nodding, like he knew the same thing
I knew but couldn't say. *Before it happens. Before
it is over.*

"I'll tell him," he said. I gave him back his tea.

"I've got to go. See you around, Bill."

"Take care," he said, looking me up and down
like he could hardly believe what I was and that
he was talking to me. And that he still liked me.
I walked away, wondering at it all.

I went to the Salvation Army for supper.
Wanted to talk to Mira. She's been giving me tips
about knife and mangler fighting. We even practice together sometimes. That woman is fast. I'm
glad she's a friend instead of an enemy. Tonight
she said something interesting.

"Don't try to fight with a Lyrri the same way
you would with anyone else."

"What do you mean?" I asked.

"Don't watch their eyes. It won't do you any
good. The only way you can knife fight with
them is to be very fast and aggressive. You won't
know where they're hitting until they're almost
home. Keep moving. And hit twice as hard as
you normally would, or your knife won't even go
in."

Yeah. Lyrri are skinny, but you never see one
with scratches or cuts. They're like diamonds.
Well, maybe not that hard.

Anyway, it was still light out after I finished
with Mira, so I took a walk. On my way around
the plaza I saw some of the new Babies. I hear
there's another School in Deadtown. Haven't got-

ten to know any of them yet. Not sure I want to.
It just isn't the same. Or maybe I just don't want
any more dead friends.

Could have scored some loki, but I had some
yesterday. I'm a lot more sensitive to it now.
Some people might think that just means I have
to build up a tolerance again, but I can feel the
difference in me. It makes me high now, just like
it did when I first tried it, and I don't want that
now.

Funny though. I can scope better than ever. I
can feel Chaz is near. It's only a matter of time.

Today it all came to a head. I'm just surprised
it didn't happen sooner. Didn't amount to much
though, thanks to Knossos.

It started in the square near the fast-food stalls.
That's the place where everything just seems to
overlap. There are always fights and always people who are happy to start them. I was cruising
the stalls, doing pretty well. I wasn't the only
one, either. Skids and Deadtowners have been
getting fat off the confusion. I'd eaten the equivalent
of two whole subs and three potato patties by
noon. I heard some yelling over in the square.

At first I thought it was just Q'rin and tinkers.
But then I heard some roars, and I knew some
lion men were into it, too.

A bunch of us got up on tables to look. Q'rins
and tinkers were fighting against Q'rins and
Aesopians. Some human-dogs were swinging at
anything that moved. It was outrageous. The people at the stalls started cheering and growling,
except for the Deadtowners and Skids, who got
real quiet.

The Lyrri leaned out of windows and balconies to watch. None of them were down near the trouble, as if they had expected it.

I saw someone breaking through the crowd in the square. It was Knossos. He was headed for the fountain, which has a base about three feet off the ground. He had just reached the base when someone fired a force gun.

Everyone froze for a second. Then some people started to run toward the square while others ran away. I prepared to jump under my table and hide there until it was all over.

Then Knossos yelled, *"Stop!"*

You could tell Knossos was used to giving orders, because everyone obeyed. Maybe if he had tried it a second later, it wouldn't have worked. Anyway, for the moment, we were all listening to him.

"I can't believe you are all willing to die now in a street brawl! A *race riot!* Soldiers don't die this way. *They die in battle, and this is no battle!! You don't even know who your real enemies are!!"*

The way he said that sent a chill up my spine. I snuck a look at the Lyrri in the windows.

"You make me ill with your drunkenness and your stupidity! We have all fought with or against each other for seventy years, some of us for hundreds of years, and look what it's earned us. Poverty! Death! *Disgrace!!* And all the while the carrion birds sit idly by and wait to pick our bones.

"If you really want to die now, draw your weapons. Shoot your friends along with your enemies, if you can tell them apart."

It was like having your father tell you you're an asshole. Heads began to droop and people laughed nervously. The Aesopians practically cringed.

"I promise you," Knossos said, "if you wait a little longer you'll know when to fight. And whom. It will be obvious."

Well, that made it official. We all knew what he meant, and it scared the hell out of everyone. Except the Lyrri, and that's even scarier.

I gazed at Knossos as he stood there like a monument. I couldn't hate him anymore. I'm not sure I ever did. He had warned me out of the Q'rin compound, and now he had risked his neck to prevent a riot. And succeeded. No, I don't have any hate left. Just a broken heart.

Knossos climbed down from the fountain as everyone started to move again—this time peacefully, if warily. I saw a lot of dazed expressions. People waking up from crowd lunacy. I got down from my table and sat on the bench. I didn't want to make any moves that could be misconstrued. People were edging away, down alleys and streets. Soon the stalls and the square were emptier than I've ever seen them in the middle of the day.

I sipped somebody's leftover coffee and thought it all over. Funny, I hardly even moved throughout the whole thing, but I was tired. I relaxed. I watched the last of the Skids raid the tables. Then I remembered the windows.

The Lyrri were still there, still watching. I searched from face to face until I found the one I knew.

Chaz smiled and gave me a little nod. I got up and walked away, in no particular direction. I wasn't about to sit there while he smiled at me like a shark.

*   *   *

It wasn't too long after the riot that Chaz finally approached me, though it took him longer than I thought it would. About a day and a half.

Probably, if I hadn't been spending so much time at the Salvation Army, it would have taken him longer. I shouldn't have been surprised to see him, that's for sure. But when he sat down across from me, I almost choked on my soup.

"You are a hard woman to track," he said. "I can't tell you the trouble I've been through."

"Don't bother," I said. "The answer is no."

He smiled sadly. "But you don't know what I want."

I thought I did. Just sitting in the same room with him scared me worse than I had dreamed it could, but I was still curious. I wanted to see what he would say.

"I hear you can't lose at the pits," he said. "I love to gamble there, but I'm afraid I'm not very good at it. In fact, I've been losing money steadily since I came to Z'taruh. I've tried to supplement my income with off-world enterprises, but they've—dried up lately."

Yeah, when he murdered his best customer, Mr. Huge. I wonder if all his business partners end up that way.

"I'm not independently wealthy, whatever you may have heard," he said. "I need to win badly. Very badly."

It was true. I was beginning to scope against my will, and he was turning into that predator I saw the first time I had scoped him. I couldn't even see how pretty he was anymore. It was like a faucet that had been leaking was suddenly turned on full blast. And over it all, I could see that he has the same sickness Conners had. Maybe worse, because Conners only lost because he was stupid. Chaz loses because he gets so wrapped up in the game he can't control himself. That's no way to win.

"You have a very bad habit," I said.

"Yes." The predator grinned. "A very bad habit."

And not one he's willing to give up. And he believes I'm the key to his success. I had been thinking he was ambitious the same way Oshrii is. I had to laugh. He didn't react. That was a little spooky.

"I don't want to be your partner, Chaz," I said.

"Please don't say no," he said. "I'll pay you well. I've rented an apartment in the Spacer Sector. You'll eat well, dress well. Doesn't that sound wonderful?"

"Chaz, no. The answer is no."

"You're not listening. I want you. The two of us will go far together."

"No."

I wanted to get up then and leave him there, but my legs would not cooperate. I was looking at his eyes. Like all Lyrri, he has black irises. It was like looking at a doll.

He whipped my glasses off so fast I didn't even see his hand coming. He tossed them on the floor.

"I don't like those," he said. "Don't cover your beautiful eyes anymore. Not around me."

Don't watch their eyes . . .

God, I was scared. And naked. But the thought of going with him was worse. I wrestled my scope back in, until he looked like himself again.

"There are Aesopians in the room," I said. "If

you touch me, I'll make a fuss. You know they hate you. You know what they'll do."

He did. His face got kind of stiff. He tried to stare me down. He's pretty damn good at it too, but I was more afraid to say yes than I was to say no. That was the bottom line.

"As far as I'm concerned," he said, "the deal is made."

Then he got up and left.

I sat there for a long time and twitched. Maybe I was in shock. All I know is that it took me a couple of hours before I could work up the courage to pick up my shades and walk outside. I was worried about where to go. There were still a lot of Aesopians around. Funny. Almost as if they were keeping an eye out for me. Though they've got no reason to.

I sort of drifted with the crowd. What else could I do? Eventually I'd have to crash for the night. But I knew I'd never get any sleep.

I got tired just the same. Tired enough to get blurry. To stop watching. And suddenly I felt something. A current of danger, like a cold pocket of air. I looked up and saw Q'rin everywhere.

I tried to move away from them, but they closed ranks on me. They didn't look at me or do anything obvious, but they wouldn't let me out, either. I couldn't see the Aesopians anymore. I had to get out of there soon, or I was going to drown, I just knew it. I almost slipped out between two of them.

Then something came down on my head and I bit the sidewalk.

I woke up in this beautiful apartment. I was alone. My shades were gone. Not that I needed that fact to tell me who was responsible.

This place is elegant, that's for sure. I've never seen such good taste. Maybe I should be flattered. Or maybe I should just jump out the window. We're ten floors up, so that would solve a lot of problems.

I waited hours to see what would happen. Nothing did, so I explored the place. Three bathrooms, three bedrooms, a huge living room, sizable kitchen, and a terrace. I took a shower. Watched dirty water pour off my body and down the drain. I used shampoo—didn't even do that at Donokh's. I brushed my teeth. I still have most of them. Good genes.

The closet in the room where I woke up is full of clothes. They looked like my size. Out of curiosity, I tried on a short, black dress with long sleeves and no back. It fit like a glove. Scary. I pulled on my dog boots instead of picking a pair of the dainty shoes lined up at the bottom of the closet. Ran my fingers through my wet hair and went to look in the mirror.

I guess I'm not so bad to look at after all.

I was trying to decide whether to take the dress off and put on my rag-wraps when Chaz came in—silently, but I knew it instantly.

He threw this notebook on the bed.

"I thought you would want this," he said. He looked me over. "Excellent choice."

"Did you read that?" I pointed to this notebook.

"No. I wrote in it once, as you recall. But I don't read."

Not *can't*, just *don't*. I think he's telling the truth. Guess it's too late anyway, if he's not. He handed me a large wad of credits.

"I've invited some people for poker tonight," he said. "I've heard you're very good at that.

You'll play, and I'll watch from the monitor in my bedroom."

A fucking monitor. He's probably watching me now.

A door chime sounded.

"Answer that," he said. "I'll see you later."

He went into his own room and closed the door. I went to let the people in. Chaz hadn't wasted time with small fry. There were three men from the Hill and two Q'rin nobles. They practically sweated money.

As usual, it was easy to win but harder to make it look right. I welcomed the work. Gave me something to do besides worry. I almost forgot Chaz was watching. Almost.

When they had gone, I just left the money on the table. I looked nervously down the hall at Chaz's room. His door creaked open, but he didn't come out.

"Well done, Shade," he said. "Take one thousand credits and fix yourself something to eat."

So he wasn't lying about paying well. But I still have a chair propped against my door tonight.

Chaz has got someone in the living room with him now, a boy maybe. Hard to tell because the voice is so young. They woke me up a little while ago with high-pitched laughter and crashing sounds, like they were rolling around tickling each other or something. I've heard stranger things, but this embarrassed me. I'm not sure why.

After a while the laughter got kind of breathy and was interrupted every now and then by long silences, and finally by panting. I thought about going into the bathroom and turning on the shower to drown out the sounds, but I decided against it. I have a feeling Chaz wants me to hear what's going on, and I don't want to let him know I'm awake.

A little while ago they started talking again, Chaz saying, "Let me, let me," and the boy saying, "No, don't!" but then moaning like he really liked it. Now he's panting, "Yes! Yes!" but he's also screaming, and the whole thing is getting too weird to listen to. I jammed the chair tighter under the door and checked the terrace door, which is locked up too. I drew the curtains so Chaz won't be able to look in at me through the glass. I don't think I could stand that.

Now the kid isn't saying "yes" anymore, but he's still screaming. I'm not sure if it's the kind of screaming some people do when they're having really good sex, or if he's being burned alive. Chaz isn't making any sound at all. I've got my back up against the door, next to the chair. I wish the kid would either come or die—soon!

Now the kid is just sobbing. And I am definitely fed up. A little while ago Chaz came to my door and called me. His voice sounded thick and horny. He kept calling "Shade? Shade?" so persistantly that there could be no doubt that I heard him. So finally he started saying, "Come out and join us, Shade. I want more from you. You'll like it. Can't you hear how much my friend likes it? I want you to watch me." And he tried the doorknob several times, making my heart stop.

Meanwhile, the kid is still sobbing. The sobs are getting weaker, though. This is going to be a long night.

Just now I heard Chaz ask the kid, "Shall we do it again?" The kid said something back to him, but it wasn't coherent. Sounded like he was talking underwater. I think he was trying to say "no." The panting has started again, but I don't think there's any doubt as to whether it's the pleasurable kind anymore.

I'm going to stand by the door with my knife in case that motherfucker tries to come in here.

I must have fallen asleep a few hours after the kid stopped crying. When I woke up, Chaz was standing over me and the chair was gone from the door. He was smiling happily and holding another dress out to me.

"Shower and put this on," he said. "After your breakfast we're going to the pits."

I looked away before he could see the expression on my face.

Out in the open I would have a chance of getting away from him. I was so scared he would figure out what I was thinking, I even convinced myself that I wasn't up to anything. I took the second of *two* unprecedented showers in two days and enjoyed myself doing it. I put on the dress— another short black thing, this time with red and silver threads shot through it—and my dog boots. Then I went out and sat down to breakfast with that jackal. Stuffed myself.

I didn't look at him. Not even a glance. And I didn't scope him, except to set up a sort of warning zone around myself. I felt every move he made just before he made it. That's what saved my life later.

We stepped outside the door of the apartment and strolled down the wide hallway to the lift. I kept playing along. We rode down ten floors and came out into an elegant lobby. Lyrri, a few Q'rin, and humans watched us pass through to the front door. The moment we stepped outside I felt Chaz reaching for me. I tried to avoid him, but he was faster than anything I'd ever seen. He grabbed my wrist and held on like a steel handcuff.

So I relaxed. I wasn't going to let him take me back to that apartment, no matter what. I was going to get away from him if it killed me.

I considered dropping my warning zone, since it had been useless, but decided against it.

We hopped a regular transport. I sat near the window, with Chaz pinning me in on the aisle side, and watched Capital go by. We passed out of sight of the Hill, into the seedier section of the Spacer Sector, and from there into Midtown. Babies and Skids stood on the street corners. The Babies already had that old-timer look. Chaz watched them like a housewife browsing the vegetable section in the supermarket.

Babies, Scarbabies, Skids, Ragnir vets, G-workers, tinkers, dogs. One big, ugly family, all incestuous and diseased. But all better than the thing I was sitting next to.

"Could you loosen your grip a little bit?" I asked him. "My hand is turning blue."

He did, but just enough to let the blood flow. Talk about muscle control. I felt him looking at me.

"Those lovely eyes," he said. "Madonna eyes. How they've haunted me since I first saw you. You look through everything, don't you Shade? You know what I am."

"Yes."

"How exciting. How very *real*. Reality is so

hard to come by, Shade. It's so easy for one to get lost in one's contemplation of abstracts. Of aesthetics."

"Like torture?" I asked, watching the Babies.

"Yes. Oh yes. Only the games are real. The games and what I see in your eyes, what they do to me."

You humans came along and ruined everything. You woke them up.

We passed through Midtown, skirted Deadtown, and finally got off at the pits. As we walked across the field, I noticed the animal show at Packrat's Plot was finally coming down. So much for their limited engagement.

At the pits, they had signs in four languages announcing the Triad for that night: three games with three rounds each. Chaz and I made our way to the Lyrri section, which has almost as good a view as the Q'rin section. It was also a good distance away from any of the Aesopians in the crowd.

I was feeling a sick sort of excitement. It seemed appropriate that I was fighting for my life at the pits, just like the real fighters. I almost felt brave.

The announcer came out and introduced the first players.

"The survivor of this round, will go on to play in the next round," he said. "His or her opponent will not be handicapped, since this is a lectrowhip round."

He didn't say that the only rule of a Triad is to kill your opponent. We all knew that.

"First round, Janni and Ket! Fifteen units to place your bet!"

Good thing the Triad is held only once a year,

or there wouldn't be any fighters left. Of course, tonight's crowd was bigger than usual, with people standing in the aisles. It was hard for the bet-takers to get around. I used the extra time to scope.

It was obvious to me that Janni had the definite edge. I turned to Chaz.

"Ket is my favorite," he was saying. "He gets so excited at the smell of blood. I could watch him forever. Janni does have an elegant style, though. Very detached."

I heard what he was saying, but I couldn't answer yet. My stomach was trying to blast its contents out my mouth. I had scoped the way he sees other people. The way I did with Knossos. Suddenly I realized why I needed to be partners with Knossos. It was more than just friendship. Knossos has the body of an animal and the soul of a king.

Chaz was an animal on the *inside*.

"Bet on Janni," I said. I could see I would have to rely on my own judgment this time around. If I tried to scope through him, I would get screwed up.

Chaz put his money on Janni. Unlike Captain Conners, he listened to me. We won that first bet, and the next five too—right into the mangler rounds. Because of my figuring. I think it might have been the one thing that gave me the most confidence that night. I was turning into a major-league scoper.

As we placed our bets for the first round of the freestyle game, I glanced across the pit and saw a familiar face. It was Donokh. He stared at me for a moment, then glanced at Chaz. When he looked back again, his eyes said, *I can't kill him. It's too soon. But if you want me to, I will anyway.*

I made myself look away. It was too painful, and too tempting. Donokh was twice as big as Chaz, but Chaz would kill him for sure. I knew that if I kept looking at him, he would come after Chaz when the fights were over. If that was going to happen, I wanted to make sure there were plenty of Aesopians around. I kept my eyes on the fights and expanded my warning field. That kept me busy until the end.

We won the last triple. Chaz and I got up. Even if his hand hadn't still been locked around my arm, I would have moved in sync with him. My warning zone was that sensitive. We moved with the crowd to the collection window. We had won a small fortune. Funny, I could see that, and it didn't matter. Money didn't matter at all.

Chaz and I walked out the front gate, toward the transports. We were surrounded by a crowd: Aesopians, Lyrri, Q'rin, humans. The whole political scene. We were about halfway to the transports when I made my move.

I drew one of my knives from under my dress and slashed Chaz as hard and fast as I could. I scored five times before he let me go. I jumped back and drew my other knife. Two-handed, my best style. Everyone moved away from us, then formed a wide circle around us.

Chaz should have been on the ground, but he was barely bleeding. A little pink stuff trickled down his throat. He gave me a sad smile.

"That wasn't nice," he said, drawing his own knives.

I had time for two quick thoughts: *Shit, I'm going to die* and *I hope I can make Knossos proud of me.* Then I lunged at him.

I'm lucky I've been off meltdown and loki for a while, or I would have been dead in that first split second. I could feel his moves coming, but I could barely dodge out of the way. As it was, I took some deep cuts. I kept moving in and dodging out, but I could already see I had lost. None of my cuts were penetrating that marble skin of his.

I could feel hundreds of eyes on me in that last second. No one cheered or booed us. No one moved. If there were bets on us, they weren't the kind you pay off in money. I knew I wouldn't get any help. I had to live or die on my own. I wondered how the hell Mira had faced a Lyrri in a knife fight and lived.

Their eyes. Don't look at their eyes.

But I did look. Straight into those doll-like, nothing-is-real eyes of his. I noticed that at least his smile was gone. But his eyes, so perfect, and serene, and—absent. . . .

I had stopped moving. He had too. He was caught up in my eyes, too.

And I lunged, plunging my right knife into his right eye; all the way in, straight into his brain. The crowd shouted, then was silent again.

Chaz didn't fall down, but the knives slipped out of his hands. Fluid and pink stuff dripped down his face.

"Shade," he said, "this is very real."

"Damn right," I said.

He grabbed my shoulders as quickly as if he hadn't been wounded. I was too stunned to react.

"I want to see your eyes," he said. "Promise you won't cover them."

And then he died. Fell like a side of beef, his good eye wide open.

I always wondered why pit fighters don't look happy when they win. Now I know. I felt like shit. I also felt people moving closer. I looked up.

All my scoping had been focused on Chaz. I hadn't realized how intensely until I looked up, turning the scope on everyone else. I was wide open.

The Lyrri looked like white panthers, tall and thin and all smiling at me. Behind them, giant dogs snarled and snapped. I saw some people who were like living rocks—the Q'rin? And some who were half-rock, half-dog.

Through these creatures strode Korbor, the elephant god. He wore armor and carried a staff. At his right walked Ashraa, the lion god; and at his left was Borrah, the bear god. When the white panthers saw the gods, they melted away through the crowd; though one of them scratched me delicately with his claws first and said, "I'm declaring blood feud, my dear. Chaz was my uncle. Isn't it exciting?"

After the panthers were gone, the dogs and the half-dogs ran away, too. It was just me, the gods, and the rock people.

Korbor put his gauntleted hands on my shoulders and said, "Rest now, Shade."

So I did. I'm not sure if he caught me before I hit the ground.

When I woke up, I was in a bed in a room I'd never seen before. Knossos was bending over me, bandaging me. There was a lion man and a bear man with him, the two pit fighters we had bet on once, and at the door stood the young elephant man I had followed to the warehouse.

"What happened to Korbor?" I asked Knossos.

He stared at me, looking almost awed. "You saw Him?" he asked.

"Yes. And Ashraa and Borrah. After I killed Chaz. They were wearing armor. Looked really impressive."

They talked to each other in Aesopian for a while, and I could tell they thought this was really something. But I had just figured out that it was them I had seen.

"What's the big deal?" I said. "I was hallucinating."

"You were scoping?" said Knossos.

"Yeah."

"I am honored."

Then they all stared at me again. It was embarrassing.

"My people saw you kidnapped," Knossos said. "We traced you to the apartment, but we found only your notebook. We feared you were dead, until we learned from the desk clerk that you had left with Chaz. We arrived just in time to see you kill him."

"Yeah," I said. "Good timing."

"You fought your own battle," he said, "and fought it well. Now I have paid my debts and redeemed my ship. It is repaired and ready for space."

"Why didn't you tell me you had a ship?" I cried. "I would have helped you pay for it!"

"My debts are not yours. My crew and I have been stranded here for ten years. We are pledged together—"

I turned my face to the wall. It was metal, and I could see the smooth seams where it had been welded together. It looked weird, but I was too busy thinking I had humiliated myself again to care.

Knossos put a pouch into my hand. It was full of money. He must have taken it off Chaz.

"Oh, well," I said. "At least I'm not poor. You don't have to worry about my anymore."

"Then you wish to terminate our partnership?" he asked.

"I do if you do."

He said, "A man must choose his allies well. Our choices on Ragnir were not so wise. Some of the Q'rin have made unwise choices, too. We shall all soon pay the price. You may be going to your death if you join us."

"Join you?"

"My crew. I was hoping you would grow into officer material some day. You have. Are you willing?"

He sounded very serious, so I gave the idea some serious thought. I had a feeling that I could die just as easily if I went anywhere else. Civil wars are messy, especially the interstellar kind.

"You're my partner," I said. "I'm not letting you out of my sight."

Knossos smiled with his eyes and extended his hand. "It's a deal," he said, and we shook on it.

Knossos turned to the others and spoke to them in Aesopian again. I heard their names. Ousa and Rorra I already knew. The young elephant man was Azren. They left us alone, and Knossos came to sit by my bed again.

"Shade, I am ashamed to face you now."

I was almost afraid to ask him. "Why?" My stomach felt weird when he looked at me that way.

"Snag told me you had become a meltdown addict two months ago. I could not make myself go to visit you, because I could not stand to see you in such a condition."

I didn't want to cry, but I couldn't help it. After a long time, I felt him patting my hand.

"I'm sorry," I said.

"I failed you, Shade. I am like the parents who leave their children to prostitute themselves on the street."

"No!"

"I wanted to help you. Even if you had never made anything of yourself I would have wanted that. It was not my place to judge you. I tried to watch out for you, but the Q'rin would have torn you limb from limb if I had taken you in then. I didn't even have a home for you. I should have worked harder."

"No," I said. "I had to do it myself. I had to kick the meltdown."

"I want to adopt you into my clan," he said, "as my daughter."

When he said that, I had to cry some more, and he patted my hand again. Finally I just threw my arms around him as far as they would go.

"They'll call you Lady Shade," he said.

I like the sound of that.

It didn't take me much longer to figure out that I was on Knossos's ship. It wouldn't have taken me even that long if the *Rescuer* weren't so enormous inside. It has to be, to accommodate ten-foot tall Aesopians. I don't have that whole big cabin to myself, though. I share with Mira. She's been teaching me to operate the weapons console.

Knossos took me on a tour of the *Rescuer* as soon as I was well enough to stand. "This is where you will live for the next several months," he said. "You might as well learn its boundaries now."

Those boundaries are considerable. The *Rescuer* holds a crew of one hundred.

"I've never seen an Aesopian warship before," I said. "Well, I might have seen a vid of one once, back when I didn't care about such things. But you were right when you said that pictures of things are not as good as the real thing."

"That was very wise of me," he agreed.

We walked through an archway on our way to the command deck. It was bordered by carvings of cobras, and at its apex was the head of a cobra man. His eyes glittered at me as if he were alive and could scope me. I've passed him many times since then, and he still bothers me.

Everywhere I looked I could see a symbolic or realistic image of the Aesopians, even in the letters and numbers on panels and consoles.

"Is Home like this?" I asked Knossos.

"Yes. Do you find it confusing?" He looked at me, and for a moment his eyes were those of the cobra man.

"No," I said. "The images never seem to overwhelm their environment." I was amazed when I heard those over-educated words coming from my mouth, but Knossos seemed pleased with me.

He touched a panel by a massive door, and it slid open to reveal the command deck. The first thing I saw was Knossos's chair. On its back was an engraving of Korbor. It wasn't a throne, but it suited him.

"Harmony is a principle we studied even before the Clan Wars," he said. "Though I'm not sure we really understood it in those days."

There were only a few officers on the deck, including Mira, who looked up from her station and gave us a brief nod. Knossos climbed the platform to his chair, where he could see everything and everyone on the deck. I followed, climbing the big steps with a lot less grace.

"What do you think?" he asked me after I had given everything a thorough scope.

"I've never been on a Q'rin ship," I said, "but this reminds me of them. The way they put things together, I mean. It's not as spartan as they like—"

"You're right," he said. "We have influenced them, and they, us. At one time, they studied at our universities. Some still do."

He sat in his chair and watched his people work while I digested that.

"When do we leave?" I asked.

"Within the week."

"What's left to do?"

"We need a few more supplies. A few more systems checked. My ship is in excellent condition."

"Is that what's taken you so long to space out of Z'taruh? Packing and stuff?"

"No. That took very little time. It was the Lord who owned our contract. He delayed the paperwork as long as he could, even after I had paid off the last of my debt. He wanted to see which way the wind was blowing before letting me off the hook. I think he is still waiting."

"Really? So, if he had just given you your receipt—"

"We would have been off this planet months ago."

We could have left before I had a chance to become a meltdown addict. Before Chaz would have caught me. Life is funny.

Knossos settled his big hand on my shoulder, but didn't look at me. "I know, Shade. I know."

We sat there like that until Mira finally called me a lazy bum and gave me something to do.

A week later we left Z'taruh. Knossos invited me to watch on the command deck, even though it wasn't my shift. I buckled into a guest chair and got ready for takeoff, my heart pounding. I peeked at the others, to see if they were as excited as me. Especially Knossos. But what I saw in his face had nothing to do with excitement.

"Let's go," he said.

The G-forces were like the struggle you go through when you're born. I was glad for the fight. I didn't hate Z'taruh, but I needed to really *feel* that I was leaving it, to have some sort of ceremony. The roar of takeoff was like music to me, the silence of space an anticlimax.

"Engage the screen," Knossos said once we were clear.

Rorra was the one who did that. Ousa and Mira were there too, and Snag in another guest chair. We all had reason to look at the green-brown ball that filled the viewscreen. It looked pretty, but no one was smiling.

I had never seen a planet during approach or departure, because Conners had never allowed me anywhere near a viewscreen or port. I had expected the planet to diminish rapidly from sight. It always did that in the vids. But it hardly seemed to change at all, even though thousands of miles were slipping past. I filed my questions away for a more appropriate time, and watched with the others.

A warning alarm snapped us all out of it.

"Q'rin ship!" Mira said, watching her own screen.

"On intercept?" said Knossos.

"No. But they're signalling us. Want to talk to them?"

"Yes." Knossos stood and faced the main screen. I was proud of the way he looked in his nobleman's clothes. The screen broke up into colored dots, and then Oshrii looked at us from the command deck of his own ship.

"You're trespassing," he told Knossos. "Leave immediately, or suffer the consequences."

"They've fired at us, Lord," Mira said. "Return fire?"

Knossos snorted. Their shots would miss us by several miles at that range. "No," he said more to Oshrii's image than to Mira. "It only encourages them.

"The next time we return to this sector, my Lord, you won't have to waste your time with warning shots."

Oshrii smiled, looking almost happy. "Understood, my Lord," he said, and signed off.

That was a couple of weeks ago. I haven't had much time for writing in this journal, lately. In fact, I'm not really sure I need to keep one anymore.

"All great generals keep journals," Knossos told me last night. "I have kept one for the last several years. All of the volumes sit in the House of Memories. That is where we will place yours."

"But I'm not a general," I said.

"That doesn't matter. Your thoughts will help those who come after you."

"But, um, some of those thoughts are kind of—you know—sort of intimate."

"Really?" said Snag, who was listening in, as usual. "Dirty stuff? Can I read it?"

But eventually Knossos talked me into putting my journal with his, on Home. That's where we're headed now. I can hardly believe it. Knossos says he has to confer with the other Lords; and with the cobra men, who evidently have talents very much like mine. Only theirs have more to do with seeing the future and the past. I'm not so sure I want to meet them.

Today, six more Q'rin ships intercepted us. But this time they were joining us. The flag ship is called the *Hammer*, and its captain is someone I thought I would never see again. He came to visit us in a shuttle, and stayed for supper.

"Donokh," Knossos greeted him graciously as the lock's inner door opened. "I'm glad to see you are commanding your uncle's ship. Abraa Torril was a great general."

"Thank you, Lord," said Donokh. "We are yours to command."

I stood there and blushed like a fool when Donokh finally turned to me. I couldn't think of anything to say.

"It's good to see you again," he said at last.

"You too," I stuttered.

We all sat down to eat together, and Donokh told us what was new on Z'taruh.

"Zorin has split with the frontier—it's official now." Zorin is the Q'rin homeworld. "We should have a few years to prepare while the Lyrri-allied fight among themselves to see who will be supreme leader."

"I bet it'll be Oshrii," I said.

"You may be right," he agreed, making me blush again when he looked at me. "In any event, more ships will be joining us soon. The remainder of the Aesopian population came with us from Z'taruh. Not one of your people remains there, Lord."

"That is good to hear," said Knossos, looking like a man who has just seen his people freed from slavery.

After that, the conversation got real technical, so I didn't listen very well. I just concentrated on not staring at Donokh. I didn't even scope him. If he was going to reject me, I didn't want it to happen when other people were looking on. Finally, I excused myself and went back to my cabin.

After an hour or so I heard a knock on my door. Mira was still on duty, so I had to open it myself. Donokh stood there, alone. I knew then that I had been a fool.

"I've told your father how I feel about you," he said.

"Oh. What did he say?"

"He said our private lives are our own, and he wishes us happiness."

"In that case, I suppose I'd better ask you in."

We had two hours of privacy before Mira was due back, and we took full advantage of it.

"I've missed you," he said as he stroked my breasts. God, how I had missed that feeling. Not to mention that body. "Come work on my ship. Be my gunner."

His hands were very persuasive. But I know where I belong.

"I'd better not," I said. "You're too distracting."

"You're being tactful," he said, kissing my nipple.

"I love you, but I can't leave Knossos again. Not ever."

He did a lot more kissing and nibbling before he answered that.

"I can live with that," he said. "It's not so different on Zorin. A husband very often has to visit his wife in his father-in-law's house."

I'm not sure if that was a proposal or not, but it was sure nice to hear. We took up the full two hours.

After Donokh had gone back to his ship, I went to see Knossos. He was sitting alone in his cabin, looking like a statue of Korbor.

"Donokh is a good man," he said before I could speak. "I approve of your choice."

"I don't want to leave you."

"As long as I live, you have a place with me, Shade."

That was a relief. I sat down next to him and looked at the star field outside his viewport. We sat there for a long time contemplating eternity. Naturally, I got bored before he did.

"Knossos," I said, "if there were no wars, what would you do for a living?"

"Where there is no conflict, there is no life," he said.

"Do you like it that way?"

He frowned, considering me with as much concentration as he had just been considering the stars. "I don't understand your question. How can one be said to like or dislike war?"

"It's just that sometimes I get the feeling things should be different. Is conflict just destruction, or is it creation, too?"

"You're beginning to get the idea," he said. "But you must understand that this question is irrelevant to the Lyrri. They'll fight this war because it's *exciting*. Perhaps they'll try to draw it out as long as they can. Do they have the weapons to destroy us at their leisure? We just don't know."

"Is that what you're hoping the cobra men can tell you?" I asked, feeling a chill up my spine at the thought.

"Yes. They have been studying the problem for years now. We are hoping for an answer soon."

He was looking tired again, but I wanted to ask one more thing. "If you could have your wish, would you wish for war or peace?"

"Peace," he said.

"Hmm. It's hard to imagine you doing a peacetime job. Like being an accountant."

"Actually," he said, "I'm quite good at keeping books."

I put my hand on his and smiled, feeling happy for the first time maybe ever. I was thinking about what he had told me once about how you have to learn to love yourself before you can do anything right. Maybe someday I'll do something right.

Just before we left Z'taruh, I went to see Mr. Field. He was in Deadtown, supervising the demolition of the first buildings. Deadtowners watched him from across the street. They finally realized what's going to happen.

Mr. Field looked at me like I was a ghost.

"My wife told me about your call two months ago," he said. "I had a feeling something was very wrong, but then you disappeared. Later Bill saw you, but—"

"I know," I said. "I'm sorry I left you in the lurch. But it was for the best. I'm leaving with Knossos now, and I wanted to say goodbye."

"Where are you going?"

"To the Aesopian homeworld. Then, probably to war."

He nodded. Behind him, tinkers were yelling at each other and climbing all over the ruins.

"How long do you think it will be before it breaks?" he asked.

"How long will it take you to finish the fortress?"

"Oshrii wants to push up the deadlines. We'll be hiring twice as many people as I thought we would. Should be about five years." He was looking at the Deadtowners and feeling bad.

"All right," I said. "Get yourself a ship as soon as the end of the project is in sight. Take your money, your wife, and whatever else you value, and head for Odin. It's cold there, so take your long underwear."

"What will happen to them?" He nodded to the people across the street.

"I don't know."

"Bet they'd make a good army."

I grinned. "Mr. Field, I sure hope you end up on the right side."

He held out his hand, and I shook it.

"See you in five years," he said.

I turned and walked away from Deadtown. I know I'll never see it again.

If you and/or a friend would like to receive the *ROC Advance*, a bimonthly newsletter featuring all the newest and hottest ROC books and authors, on a complimentary basis, please fill out this form and return it to:

ROC Books/Penguin USA
375 Hudson Street
New York, NY 10014

Your Address
Name _____
Street _____ Apt. # _____
City _____ State _____ Zip _____

Friend's Address
Name _____
Street _____ Apt. # _____
City _____ State _____ Zip _____